HENRY &
THE INCREDIBLY INCORRIGIBLE,
INCONVENIENTLY INTELLIGENT
SMART HUMAN

L.A. MESSINA

TATER TOT BOOKS
A Division of Potatoworks Press
Greenwich Village

For information about Tater Tot Books,
please visit www.potatoworks.wordpress.com.

For Emmett Thompson Catanese,
the first ETC and the most incredible

CONTENTS

HENRY &
THE INCREDIBLY INCORRIGIBLE,
INCONVENIENTLY INTELLIGENT
SMART HUMAN

CHAPTER ONE
LANK HANK TANKED

No, no, no, Henry thought as the buzzing started. It was only a gentle *wzzz-wzzz* vibration now, but it would spread quickly, coursing through his circuits until it became a full-blown rattle that would shake his entire robot frame. If he didn't stop the *wzzz* now, this instant, he would lose power and crumble to the floor like a soggy piece of paper.

No!

Henry was in the middle of an important exam, but he didn't care. He closed his textbook-reading and word-processing applications. The only way to stop the *wzzz* and avoid total system crashdown was to shut as many applications as possible.

"I'll repeat the question," said Mrs. Yitteriumski, his thirteenth-upgrade teachbot, after an extended silence.

"Modern electrology believes that complex circuitry evolved from simpler circuitry by the method of informed selection. Explain informed selection."

Henry was being tested on information retrieval. One week ago, he'd gotten his thirteenth upgrade, which included two new drives. Now he had to demonstrate—in front of the whole class—how well he could find information on the new drives.

In the back row, Sissy O'Thalium snickered.

The *wʒʒʒ* kicked up.

He closed his dictionary app, his way-finding app and his weather-predicting app.

"You have one minute, Henry," Mrs. Y said.

Henry didn't need a reminder. His own internal clock marked each second faithfully.

Wʒʒʒ-wʒʒʒ.

He closed his time-keeping app.

Despite appearances—the same shiny metallic frame, the same two legs, same two arms, same round head—Henry Jacobson wasn't like the other students in Mrs. Yitteriumski's thirteenth-upgrade class. He had a severe system error. It dated back to his seventh upgrade, when a virus had been uploaded to his C drive. The bug rooted itself in his memory, consuming more and more megabytes each time he opened a new app until he had nothing left to run his system and he crashed.

The first time it happened, he'd been in the middle of an exam just like this one. He had been showing his teachbot that he knew how to control his feelings using his newly upgraded emotionality stabilizer. He successfully downgraded several extreme emotions—euphoric to happy, despondent to sad, irate to angry—but while he was in the middle of reducing petrified to scared, the world suddenly went black. One moment there was light; the next darkness washed over him.

He woke on the floor with the entire class staring down at him, pointing, smirking, whispering. He heard Sissy say, "Lank Hank."

Of course, he was rushed to the hospital. After a week of running diagnostics on all his systems—ventilation, circuitlation, operating—the doctors finally found the virus hiding in his logic board. They overwrote the code and performed an emergency RAM upgrade, but they couldn't remove the entire virus. A tiny part of it—the *wᴢᴢᴢ-wᴢᴢᴢ*—stayed behind.

"Thirty seconds, Henry," Mrs. Y said, her voice modulator turned to TALKING TO A DISOBEDIENT CHAIR.

So now he was stuck with the choice between failing his midterm or crashing in front of the whole class.

Henry closed his letter-recognizing app.

"Thank you, Henry," Mrs. Y said, dinging softly once. A lone ring meant failure. "You can return to your seat."

In the six years since he'd caught the bug, he'd gotten used to the lone ding of failure. Still, it was better than the dull roar of humiliation. So what if he had a reputation as a slacker and was grouped with robots with slow processors?

"Sissy," Mrs. Y called, "please come to the front of the class and access the information."

Sissy smirked and stood up. As she passed Henry in the aisle, she said, "Lank Hank tanked."

The teachbot's sound sensors failed to pick up the comment, but everyone else in the class heard it loud and clear; the snickers followed him to his seat.

"Informed selection," Sissy said, her voice modulator turned to TEACHBOT'S PET. "Over the course of generations, the robot species evolved by identifying and choosing those applications that best aided in its survival and integrating them in the next generation. Populations with sloppy code were phased out while populations with elegant code thrived. In this way, robots developed from simpler machines like calculators. The fossil record bears this out, and science has demonstrated conclusively that the modern *machinicus roboticus* shares 92 percent of its circuitry with *machinicus calculus*."

Mrs. Yitteriumski beamed with pride as Sissy demonstrated that her recently upgraded textbook-reader application on her new E drive was properly scanning words and processing their meanings.

"Excellent," the teacher said. "Discuss the theory of primordial buzz."

Henry's wires flickered in disgust. Who couldn't find primordial buzz? It was in chapter six, on the F drive, and now that he wasn't under any pressure—no scornful classmates, no impatient teachbots—he could easily access it.

Sissy could, too. "The theory of primordial buzz seeks to explain the origin of life on our planet, Ferrous, and to hypothesize where the first single-circuit organism came from. Dr. Samuel Goldberg proposes a 'primordial buzz' of solar winds, electromagnetic fields, lightning storms and static electricity combined at the right moment to create charges, which combined in ever more complex ways until they formed currents, which in turn combined and ultimately formed circuits."

Mrs. Y chimed eight times, one more than the highest score of A++.

Great, so now Sissy got extra points for just repeating stupid data files.

Sissy gave Henry a superior look as she took her seat and immediately began passing notes with her best friend, Chrissy. Like all modern robots—and Henry himself—they were created from an advanced metal alloy that made all their movements incredibly smooth and graceful, as opposed to the jerky fits and starts of their great-great-great grandparents.

Thanks to advances in alloy, the modern robot could express up to fifty-three different emotions, including smug, despondent and lost, whereas previous generations could produce only the basics such as happy, sad and angry. Likewise, they had more options for expressing themselves verbally, as the thirteenth upgrade contained 287 new voice modulations. It also came with improvements in their aesthetic, pain-tolerance and art-appreciation protocols.

Different robot models were made from different alloys. Sissy was a Zilly 3.5 made of nisil. Mrs. Y was a Zagnet 23 made from doré bullion. Henry was a Zaklad 5000 made from stellite, a highly stain-resistant alloy that gave his silver frame a nice reflective sheen. His sight sensors were thick orbs that glowed green when he was happy and spun in their sockets when he was annoyed. His smell sensor was a square bump in the middle of his face. To his mother's dismay, it was a half-inch off center, which gave him a perpetually confused look as if he were always smelling something not in his scent database. His verbalizor was a thick slash that gradually got thinner at the edges for maximum sound production, and two little perfect balls on each side of his head captured and deciphered the clamor and clatter of everyday noise.

Mrs. Y called on her next victim, and Evan Leadbetter shuffled to the front of the classroom. "Explain the difference between an independent mineralizor and a dependent mineralizor."

Evan's sight sensors tilted down, as if the answer were written on the floor instead of on his hard drive. While he struggled to find the file, Sissy and Chrissy openly passed notes. They did it all the time, and Mrs. Y never noticed. It was as if her sight sensors couldn't register the two girls. It was so unfair. Henry knew if he had a best friend to pass notes with, they'd get caught in an instant.

Sissy knew it too and smiled smugly at him when she saw him looking. Embarrassed, Henry immediately glanced down. "Do you want to know what it says?" she whispered, holding out a piece of folded paper, the new technology that made passing notes practically undetectable. The old method of sending electrode bleeps emitted waves that a teacher's wave-detecting app immediately trapped and deciphered.

He ignored her and focused on pulling up the information Evan was struggling to access. Independent mineralizor: a machine that could produce all the calcium it needed to grow. Examples included robots, sedanmobiles and jetcrafts. These machines were mobile and able to move freely. Dependent mineralizor: a machine that drew calcium from the ground. Examples included consolis, digitalis and lamps. These machines were rooted to one spot and couldn't move.

"Go on, take it," Sissy said.

"No," Henry muttered. He couldn't care less about their stupid scribblings. It was probably some boring note about what they were going to do after school or a snide comment about Mrs. Y.

"Don't be afraid. It won't hurt you."

"I'm not interested," Henry said.

Mrs. Y looked at him sharply. "Your attitude, Henry, explains why you did so poorly on your practical exam. Perhaps you'll be interested in detention. See me after school."

Sissy and Chrissy giggled loudly but weren't reprimanded or ordered to stay late. If anything, Mrs. Y nodded at them approvingly.

It was *so* unfair.

Henry spent the rest of the afternoon seething silently. Some robots could do whatever they wanted and never get in trouble and other robots barely said a word and got detention for the rest of their lives. The lack of fairness bugged him so much, he barely noticed when the 3 o'clock bell rang.

Slowly, Henry stood and zipped up his fannypack. Every robot wore a little pack midway up his frame, right above the fan in his ventilation system, to carry things like pens, money, snacks and portable communicators. Henry's everyday fannypack was black with the logo of his favorite video game, *Mission Commander,* but when he went to his after-school job at the Shine Bar Spa & Boutique he had to change into a pink one that said I TOOK A SHINE TO THE SHINE BAR in bright purple.

Every time he put it on, he felt the sharp sting of mortification before his emotionality stabilizer downgraded it to embarrassment.

"Don't forget, Henry," Mrs. Y called, as he pushed in his chair, "we have an appointment. You can start with the blackboard. Sponges and purification fluid are in the cabinet."

Sissy giggled once more as she threw her bag over her shoulder. "Lank Hank spanked!" she quipped on her way out.

Grumbling, Henry tried to decide which he hated more—the *wzzz-wzzz* or Sissy O'Thalium.

CHAPTER TWO

SHELF THE PUT. BOTTLE THE MOP.
LID THE CLEAN. JARS THE STOP.

Thanks to detention, Henry arrived fifty-seven minutes and twenty-five seconds late for his after-school job. His boss—his mom!—docked him two hours' pay and sent him straight back to the storeroom to help the human unit unpack a recent shipment of Dr. FeelGoodiums Medical Marvel Degrooving Cream.

"Punctuality is actuality," she called at his departing back as he grumbled about unfair working conditions.

The Shine Bar Spa & Boutique was a full-service beauty salon located on Disk Drive, in the center of Sodium Falls' tidy shopping district—a five-block stretch in the downtown area with wide sidewalks and arching pink stalagmite tree formations. In its six treatment rooms and ten beauty stations, the Shine Bar offered more than a dozen procedures, including waxing, dent amelioration, buffing, shining and realignment. Each beauty treatment was administered by a beautybot specially programmed in its protocols.

Henry knew working in a beauty salon was the twelfth level of not cool—Evan Leadbetter sold tickets at the movie theater two blocks down—but the money was good and the pace was fast. His job was to make sure all the bottles were filled and the equipment cleaned and returned to its proper place. Henry frequently spent the afternoon darting from one end of the salon to the other, half-empty jars clutched in his fingers. It required a lot of memory and advanced organizational skills to keep the lotions and potions and tools and utensils straight, plus a quick processor to respond to the many demands and commands of clients and beautybots.

Although he'd never admit it, Henry enjoyed being there. Sometimes he got to run the cash register at the Boutique counter, where his mom sold signature lotions and fannypacks, and that was actually fun. Plus, he liked the feel of the space—the wide aisles, the high ceilings, the crystal chandeliers that scattered rainbows along the white walls and floor tiles. It was very different from his home, which was decorated according to his mother's design app's default setting of midcentury cluttered.

Henry also liked his coworkers. Everybot was really nice.

Except his mother.

Jane Jacobson was a top-of-the-line Zolot 5.0 managerial model. After getting straight A++ through high school, she went on to university, where she mastered all the specialized apps for a career in upper management.

It was perfect for her. Jane was only happy when she was telling other bots what to do.

Like now. Go help the human unit unpack boxes, Henry.

Yes, ma'am.

Henry opened the door to the storeroom and found the human sitting in the center of the shelf-lined room. It was unpacking the boxes per its instructions, but the unit hadn't stopped there. It'd opened each jar and dumped the

8

contents on the concrete floor. Globs of gray goo oozed slowly in every direction.

"Great," Henry muttered, examining the mess. For a modern convenience, the CRZ78BX-22 Drudgery was awfully *in*convenient.

To be fair, the CRZ was an old model, so old its manufacturer didn't even make the Drudgery line anymore. Typically, a human unit went to the compaction facility after four years. Human technology improved quickly, and each successive generation had a larger dictionary, more storage, improved scanning skills, a greater ability to remember commands and increased emotional stability. The spa's human had almost no memory, little storage, nonexistent deciphering skills and a fifty-word vocabulary.

But even the newer models were hardly the height of productivity their maker claimed. Forty years after HueManTech introduced the first human appliance, the Smith 100-X-1, the technology had yet to catch up with the company's slogan: "Humanity—the solution you've been waiting for."

HueManTech—the leading manufacturer of human units and human products and accessories—insisted that one day Dr. Felix J. Tinsmith's famous invention would be able to do everything a robot could, including processing independently and thinking freely. For now, though, it could only sweep floors and take out trash.

And the Shine Bar's human couldn't even do those minimal tasks.

"Clean up this mess," Henry said, closing the door behind him. He didn't want his mom to see the glop-covered floor. He knew she'd blame him whatever the circumstance.

The human tilted its head up, its stringy hair falling over its sight sensors, and looked at Henry—although *looked* was overstating the case. Its sight sensors, which were a leaden muddy-brown color, stared in his general direction without actually seeing him. There was no sign of recognition in its droopy lips and sunken cheeks.

Although the CRZ78BX-22 didn't respond, its sight sensors blinked, so Henry knew the device hadn't crashed, or, as the manufacturer called it, fainted.

Fainting was a fail-safe built into the human's system to prevent cases of berserkoness, a malfunction in which the unit has a complete system break. Berserkoness was a product of the human unit's unstable emotionality platform. Without an emotionality stabilizer, a human had no way of controlling its feelings and frequently suffered from emotional extremism, a malfunction that could render it unusable for days.

The problem had been largely fixed in newer models, and you rarely heard of a unit going berserko these days— although every so often you flipped on the evening news and heard about a unit trying to throw its owner in the trash.

"Clean up this mess now," Henry repeated.

The CRZ didn't respond.

The secret to successfully operating a human was to provide simple, detailed instructions. It wasn't enough to tell it to sweep the salon. You had to tell it to go to the storeroom at the back of the spa, open the door, pick up the mop, dip it into cleaning fluid and wash the floor. Some units needed even more precise directions—for example, to turn the knob on the door. Otherwise, it would bump its head against the door over and over as it tried to get into the storeroom.

Henry gave the order again, this time using human command code. "Put the lids back on the jars, put the bottles on the shelf, pick up the mop and clean the floor." He spoke slowly as he fetched the mop from the back wall.

The human watched him, its glassy-eyed stare steady and empty. Then suddenly it emitted a noise, a low rumble that seemed to emanate from its trunk. Surprised, Henry listened, realizing only as the sound turned into a high-pitched wail that the Drudgery unit was laughing. The act itself seemed to take over its entire frame, and the human clutched its middle, as if trying to hold in the sound. Droplets of water fell from its sight sensors.

Henry was annoyed. Wailing and crying usually preceded a faint, and he didn't want to wait ten or twenty minutes for the unit to reboot.

But instead of falling to the floor, the human darted

out a hand and grabbed the mop. "Shelf the put. Bottle the mop," it said. "Lid the clean. Jars the stop."

"Yes," Henry said, relieved by this demonstration of functionality.

The unit stood, clutching the mop. "Shelf the put. Bottle the mop. Lid the clean. Jars the stop."

Henry nodded encouragingly. "Great. But start with the jars first. Put the lids back on the jars, then put the jars on the shelf, *then* clean the floor."

The unit continued to repeat the garbled instructions, but it seemed to understand what it was supposed to do. At the very least, it recognized the word *mop*.

Satisfied with the unit's progress, Henry darted to the door to make his escape. If he wasn't around when the human made a mess of the cleanup, he couldn't be blamed for it. Instead, he'd go to the staff lounge and straighten the cushions on the couch. The break room was always a mess.

While he was there, he could maybe snag a few CoalSnaps. CoalSnaps, gritty balls of resolidified capacitated coal, were his favorite snack. They tasted yummy, and a handful popped into his energy pit—a narrow opening under his left shoulder (aka the coal hole)—would give him enough energy to make it to dinner.

His reactor coil could definitely use some refueling right about now.

Henry had just grabbed the knob when the door was suddenly and violently struck by the long wooden handle of the mop. Amazed, Henry spun around and stared at the human. It stared back, muddy-brown eyes aglow with excitement, its entire frame shaking with laughter. In a single, unprecedentedly graceful movement, it swung the mop high over its head and brought it down on the floor a mere inch from Henry's foot.

"Shelf the put. Bottle the mop. Lid the clean. Jars the stop," it said, raising the mop again. "Shelf the put. Bottle the mop. Lid the clean. Jars the stop."

Immediately, Henry's hazard meter initialized and read the situation as POSSIBLY HAZARDOUS, which was a little worse than MAYBE HAZARDOUS but not as bad as

PROBABLY HAZARDOUS. Before the program could go all the way to DEFINITELY HAZARDOUS, the human stalked out of the room, wielding its mop.

"Shelf the put. Bottle the mop. Lid the clean. Jars the stop," it repeated, storming through the Shine Bar breaking mirrors and bottles and lights. It took three swings at the dent ameliorator before knocking the fragile machine to the floor, where it smashed into a hundred little pieces. "Shelf the put. Bottle the mop. Lid the clean. Jars the stop."

The sense of panic was slow to start. The sound of breaking glass wasn't all that unusual at a salon, and everyone assumed a buff 'n' shine bot had dropped a bottle. But then Mrs. Nobiumfeld caught sight of the Drudgery's maniacal grin in the mirror a second before it was shattered by the handle of the mop. She screamed; the human chanted; pandemonium broke out.

Chairs were overturned as clients jumped to their feet midtreatment and raced to the door, unconcerned about the tints, waxes, foils and creams still coating their frames. Panicked shrieks filled the air as patrons tripped over each other in a mad dash to the street.

Henry's mom tried to control the chaos. "Please exit the building in an orderly fashion," she said calmly. "Safety for one means safety for all."

Nobot listened, not even her staff, who were trained in emergency evacuation procedures. The horde poured out onto the sidewalk in one screeching gush, and in less than a minute, only she, Henry and the berserko human unit remained. A crash tore through the salon as the mop decimated the end table in the waiting area. Henry felt his hazard meter inch upward to LIKELY HAZARDOUS.

"Henry, please exit the building in an orderly fashion," his mom called, her tone still calm despite the berserko unit pulverizing her waiting room.

There was a back door through the storeroom, and although he could easily escape, running out would mean leaving his mom alone with the crazed human. His ethics app concluded that wasn't the ethical response. His gaze swept the room, searching for a weapon. The chair? He could toss it at the CRZ78BX-2. He initialized his vector-measuring app to gauge the right angle.

The *wzzz-wzzz* hummed softly through his frame.

Henry closed the vector app.

He looked for something that wouldn't require him to open an application as the Drudgery unit smashed the chandelier over the reception station and shards of glass rained down on his mother. Jane Jacobson curled in a ball to protect her sensors from the falling debris. When she stood up, she had a long electrical cord in her hand. She swung it over her head like a lasso and with a flick of her wrist sent it flying. It whipped through the air and over the human's shoulders. She pulled once tightly, trapping the human's arms to its sides. She pulled again and the unit toppled to the floor. With the rest of the cord, she expertly trussed up the deranged appliance and stuffed a rag in its mouth to stop the demented chant.

Henry watched, amazed. How could his mother *possibly* know how to do that? She was the manager of a beauty parlor in the suburbs, not a G-bot for the Federal Agency of Observation and Reportation.

His mom, standing with one foot on the human unit's chest, looked at him disapprovingly. "I kindly requested that you exit the building in an orderly fashion," she said. "In the future, I trust you'll comply with all parental commands."

Henry wanted to protest the unfairness of that particular command, but he was too in awe of his mother to do anything but stare. The way she threw that cord....

As if scanning his microchip, Jane said, "I'm programmed to neutralize any and all possible threats, including shoplifters, saboteurs from rival salons and marauding vacuum cleaners. Now, are you ready to go?" Henry nodded, and his mom tugged the cord, bringing the human to its feet. "Good, on the way home we'll drop this thing off at the compaction facility to be compressed and boxed for the landfill. What would you like for dinner? I was thinking pot roast."

Still stunned, Henry nodded again. As he did, the *wzzz-wzzz* slowly died, but the feeling that he was completely useless because of his stupid system error stayed with him.

CHAPTER THREE

NEW AND IMPROVED
CEREBRAL CORTEXTINATOR™!

The Jacobsons lived at 27 Hard Drive in a white clapboard house along a street lined with ragged pink stalagmites and other white clapboard houses. Their lawn was a well-kept field of green tourmaline crystal, dutifully shaved smooth every Sunday by Henry's father. It was bordered by a neat row of dusk-blooming nightlights. His mother loved their soft glow and planted bulbs every spring.

It was autumn now, but the weather rarely changed in Sodium Falls. It was always clear and seventy, optimal conditions for a bot to thrive. Other regions had crippling rainstorms that kept whole communities inside for days.

Water was extremely harmful to robots, and although most logic boards could withstand a light sprinkle, a downpour fried the whole system. All schoolchildren were taught a rhyme to keep them safe: A drizzle won't sizzle. A shower has power. A torrent is abhorrent.

For this reason, all robots checked their weather app several times a day, kept a fully laminated RainRescue SlickGuard in their fannypack and hoped for the best.

Jane pulled her car into the driveway behind her husband's, an Esperzo 2167¾ sedanmobile still revving furiously from the drive home. The Esperzo, with its slick, low-to-the-ground frame, red racing stripes and loud growl, was a sportier model than Jane's practical gray Ergmenty 1.0, but it was harder to handle. The sleek machine, from the wilds of the Vast Open Space of the Very Far West, was barely tamed and reacted to only the strongest of commands, which meant that Henry's father, Jacob, was always yelling at it. In contrast, the locally grown Ergmenty responded to the slightest request. All his mother had to do was say, "Stop. Park. Sleep," and the car was in for the night.

As soon as the Ergmenty paused, Henry jumped out. He ran up the walk and burst through the front door. "You won't believe what happened," he announced excitedly. "Mom's human completely lost it! Banged up the spa! Broke every mirror and trashed the chandeliers! Mrs. Nobiumfeld totally freaked. All Mom's clients did and the staff too. It was fantastic."

Henry was halfway into the room before he noticed his dad's boss, Mr. Marcus Erickson, sitting on the couch across from Jacob. He screeched to a halt. "Good evening, sir," he said politely but with a curious look at his dad. Although he had met Mr. Erickson at various company functions over the years, this was the first time the bossbot had been in their home.

Erickson got to his feet. "Hello, Henry," he said, then greeted Jane just as warmly as she entered behind her son.

Jacob stood up too. "Mr. Erickson dropped by," he explained, stating the obvious as he fiddled with the zipper on his fannypack.

Both things struck Henry as unusual—his father never made unnecessary comments and he always removed his fannypack upon arriving at home.

Something was up.

"I'm terribly sorry to hear about your human," Erickson said. "It's appalling that these so-called technologists can't fix a simple problem like berserkoness. I hope you didn't find the experience too distressing. Everybot seems to be unharmed," he added, looking from her to Henry and back again.

Jane assured him that, yes, everyone got out safely. "But my staffed failed to follow protocols and my clients were terrified. I'm going to lose business to the Polish Palace over this unless I do something drastic."

"You could have a Sorry Our Human Went Crazy sale," Henry suggested.

His mother's pleasantly neutral expression dipped into disapproval at the comment, but Mr. Erickson laughed appreciatively.

Henry's wires buzzed in delight. From the very first moment he'd met him, Henry had liked his father's boss. Mr. Erickson was a busy man, but he always found time to say hello to him on the rare occasions Henry visited the office. And last year at the company picnic, Erickson played a full round of mini-golf with him. What's more, he let Henry win.

Henry couldn't say what, but something about Mr. Erickson reminded him of his dad. Both were tall, over six feet, but that was all they had in common. Erickson was a late-model Zolot—wide, boxy and made of a beryllium-copper alloy. He had over sixty-five upgrades under his fannypack, and his burnished-bronze frame showed more than a hint of green oxidation (an inevitable sign of aging, as was loss of smoothness in the joints, but nothing Jane couldn't take care of in three easy treatments).

In contrast, Jacob, a Zstad 29, was sleek, aerodynamic and made of a blue-tinted, wear-resistant alloy.

Maybe the reason they seemed similar was they both let him win. Mr. Erickson did it because he was nice and his father because he wanted to avoid an unpleasant scene. Despite his many upgrades, Henry was still a sore loser.

"Thank you, Henry, for the suggestion," his mother said politely. Henry knew she wanted to say something more censorious, but her managerial programming and etiquette protocols prevented her from chastising him in front of his father's boss. "Now, Mr. Erickson, what can I get you? I was just about to roast some coal for dinner. Please say you'll stay."

Erickson smiled. "You are too kind to offer, but as much as I would like a home-capacitated meal, I'm afraid this isn't a social call. I have a very important business matter to discuss."

If Jane thought it was strange that her husband's boss chose to hand out an important assignment after work and away from the office, she didn't indicate it. She merely wrapped an arm around Henry's shoulders. "Then we'll get out of your way and let you continue."

"Please stay," Erickson said. "And Henry, too."

Excited to participate in his very first business meeting, Henry slipped free of his mother's arm and planted himself firmly on the couch. In contrast to the Shine Bar's sleek simplicity, the Jacobsons' living room—and indeed the whole house—was a riotous mix of colors and patterns. Every surface was covered with a colorful design: plaid on the couch, swirls on the walls, mining scenes on the drapes. A small army of three-inch knitted figurines—knitted by Jane herself in her spare time—marched across the room and the rest of the house.

Jacob and Jane lowered onto the couch next to Henry as Erickson pulled up the armchair.

"Don't tell anyone else in the office," he said confidingly to Henry, "but your father is my best employee."

This confession didn't surprise Henry in the least. Jacob Jacobson took his job as the head of the Upgrade Processing Department very seriously. The UPD oversaw application distribution for all the robots in the country, which meant making sure the right robot got the right apps for his or her function. Without this oversight, bots would be able to change their programming whenever they wanted. Sanitation bots could become physicist bots and chiropractor bots could become welder bots and botanist bots could become detective bots.

The delicate balance of the universe would be destroyed.

Chaos would ensue.

As head of the Central Process Unit, Erickson supervised the UPD as well as two other departments—Network Processing and Generation Processing. Network Processing reviewed requests for male and female robots to link up, or network, a state often called marriage by the government employees who regulated the transactions. Generation Processing oversaw the production of the next generation of robots. Almost exclusively submitted by networked couples, next-generation requests outlined what kind of robot the couple planned to make and what traits each partner would be contributing.

The CPU was an important branch on the Circuit Tree, the administrative arm of the United Territories of Greater Vanadium government. The Motherboard made the laws and bots like Erickson and Jacob at the Circuit Tree implemented them. The Mainframe—the third arm of government—made sure everybot followed the laws.

Jacob Jacobson, who was raised in an orphanage after his widowed mother was killed by thugbots that broke into her home, never expected to have such an important job. Robots with state educations usually wound up as low-level swatters at a telemarketing firm or an insurance company, which is what happened to Jacob. After a two-month search, he finally got a job as a claims processor for Happy Safe Robot Insurance ("We keep robots happy and safe!"). Processors cleaned up code littered with bugs, which was dull, tedious, repetitive work that any vacuum with half a microchip could do. For that reason, they were called swatters. Processor bots sat at their desks and swatted flies all day.

He would have remained at Happy Safe Robot his whole life, rusting slowly, if Mr. Marcus Erickson hadn't somehow found him in the company's poorly ventilated basement and offered him a spot in the CPU. Jacob, who never dreamed of a cushy government assignment, couldn't believe his luck.

Fifteen years later, he still loved his job, even though it was considerably more draining now that he ran the department.

"And as my best employee," Erickson continued, "he is the only one I would trust with an assignment of this importance."

Jacob nodded his head respectfully. "Thank you, sir."

"In the trunk of my hatchbackmobile, I have the very latest in robotoid technology," Erickson announced. "Your task is to run the ETC-420-GX-2 through its paces and keep a log of how it performs."

Henry didn't know what *robotoid* meant, but at the mention of the word, he felt his mother stiffen. She didn't speak, of course, as protocol would never permit her to interrupt her husband's boss, but Henry could hear her circuits whirring.

Jacob opened his fannypack, then closed it again with a firm zip. "Thank you, sir, I'm very honored to be chosen as well as flattered that you think so highly of my skills. However, as much as I would like to accept the assignment, I don't think I'm the right bot for the job. We've never had a human in our house. We don't think technology is an acceptable substitute for good old-fashioned parenting," he explained, referring to the common practice of plopping a babybot in front of a nanny unit for hours on end. Humans were popular as caretakers for pre-upgraders because their memory, language and cognitive abilities were exactly the same. Botties could stare for hours at a human's blinking eyes. "Given the circumstance, I wouldn't be able to provide an accurate accounting of its performance."

"A human?" Henry asked, jumping to his feet. "We're getting a human?" All the other kids at school had them.

His mother tugged him back down to the couch.

"In addition, sir, I don't think this is the right time for a human. Henry just survived a harrowing attack from one," Jacob said.

Erickson blinked one purple sight sensor at the young bot in question. "You weren't harrowed, were you, Henry?"

"Oh, no. Not at all, sir," he said eagerly. "It was like being in a MegaBot comic. Pow! Bam! Boom! Take that, you berserko human!" he said, punching the air.

Jane beeped warningly. Henry folded his hands in his lap.

"As well, Henry just underwent his thirteenth upgrade," Jacob added. "You know how difficult an experience that can be."

His disgust meter launched and registered QUITE DISGUSTED, as Henry rolled his sight sensors. Of *course* his dad pulled the old thirteenth-upgrade excuse out of his fannypack. His parents were so predictable.

Yes, the thirteenth was the hardest one of all. Yes, you had to integrate 764 new programs into your operating system, which was *double* the usual number. And, yes, this presented a risk for all robots, not just the ones with a disability. The thirteenth was a turning point: the moment when you finally had all your standard apps but not the skills to fully control them. Everybot found the change difficult, but some never made the adjustment. Instead, they crashed over and over again, their logic boards frying, until they were a frame with nothing but dead circuitry inside—an empty, a tin can, a deader. It was every parent's nightmare.

But that didn't mean his folks had to initiate their treat-Henry-like-a-helpless-little-botty app. Just because he *wzzz*ed-out sometimes didn't mean he was about to crash permanently.

"I'm fine. I haven't had an episode in almost a year," Henry said, tactfully leaving out the fact that he was almost flunking out of school as a result. "I handled today, didn't I?"

"You didn't obey my order to leave the building," his mom said.

Henry folded his arms and grumbled that he wasn't going to run to safety while his mom was in danger like some sissy fifth-upgrader. His dad looked at him approvingly. "Disobedience isn't a sign of system malfunction."

"And he failed his information-retrieval practical and got detention," Jane added.

Henry *knew* she'd use that against him.

Jacob looked at him with an expression of keen disappointment, and Henry feared he was about to hear about his father's disadvantaged youth again. Mastering new applications was a major part of the national curriculum; only those robots who performed all their functions perfectly on command went on to top universities, where they specialized in a particular profession. The rest became low-level swatters.

"What do I always say, Henry?" his dad asked.

And here we go.

"Keep your smell sensor to the grindstone," Henry said, embarrassed to be running through this routine in front of Mr. Erickson.

Jacob nodded. "Keep your smell sensor to the grindstone. Focus on the goal. What's the goal, Henry?"

"Good grades," he muttered.

"Excellent grades," Jacob corrected.

"That is correct, Jacob," Erickson said, leaning forward in his chair. "Excellent grades are vital for social advancement. You must study hard, Henry, and pay careful attention in school. The ETC-420-GX-2 will help him do that by freeing up his time for homework and exam prep. It has a new and improved cerebral cortextinator that has virtually eliminated the issue of emotionality. According to my OddOdds program, there is only a 1 in 643,669.08 chance of this robotoid model suffering berserkoness."

"I don't doubt it, sir, but I don't think we're the right family for this project," Jacob said. "Perhaps you can assign it to someone else with more experience using human technology."

Erickson nodded. "I wish I could, Jacob, but the Motherboard asked for you specifically."

Both Jacob and Jane shot to their feet. "What!" they cried in unison.

The branch manager leaned back in his chair. "Yes, that's exactly what happened. You see, this assignment is part of a joint initiative with the HueManTech corporation to create a regular generalist model for middle-class families," he explained. "The government is considering offering a surcharge credit to help make this model more affordable, but before doing so they have to determine if it's appropriate for an average Vanadiumian family. You have been chosen to ascertain its suitability."

Jacob's wires buzzed as he tried to process the information. "The Motherboard asked for *me* by name?"

Jane seemed to be having the same problem. "You're saying that out of the 94,612 robots working at the 569 branches of the Circuit Tree, the Motherboard asked for Jacob *specifically*?"

Erickson smiled and winked at Henry, who smothered a giggle. "Yes, that's exactly what I'm saying."

Stunned, Jane sank back into the couch.

Jacob zipped and unzipped his fannypack three times before saying, "How?"

"You've distinguished yourself with your overwhelming averageness," Erickson explained.

Jacob's eyes flashed as he reached down to grasp his wife's hand. "Did you hear that, Jane? I've distinguished myself with my overwhelming averageness."

Jane smiled. "I'm so proud, Jacob."

Henry's disgust meter shot straight to OVERWHELM-INGLY DISGUSTED. Who cared *why* the Motherboard knew his father's name. All that mattered was *which* member of the Motherboard knew it.

"Was it Nickelby?" he asked excitedly.

Erickson glanced at him in surprise. "Excuse me?"

"Was it Mission Commander Nickelby who asked for my dad? Do you know him? What's he like? Will he come here? Can I meet him?"

As the young bot rattled off a torrent of questions, the CPU branch manager's facial-expression application seemed to briefly malfunction. It cycled through twenty-seven different expressions in eight seconds, landing the longest on FEAR before settling into AMUSEMENT.

"Yes, it was, Henry," he said, his voice modulator turned to the very cheerful OUR TEAM WON! setting. But it glitched too and dipped briefly into RUN FOR YOUR LIFE. "It was Mission Commander Nickelby."

Henry's emotionality stabilizer smoothly downgraded exuberant exhilaration to mildly giddy glee as he ran the likelihood of meeting Nickelby through his OddOdds program. Previously, the app had returned 1 in 2,596,004. Now it was down to 1 in 936, 276.

Whoo-hoo.

Mission Commander Nickelby was Herbert Nickelby, national hero and the first and only winner of the Vanadiumian Metal of Distinction. Forty years ago, as the president of HueManTech, he single-handedly brought down the Robothood of Peace, a terrorist organization devoted to destroying all traces of human technology, which the group thought too dangerous to exist. Henry had all six of his video games: *Mission Commander Scout Squad* 1 through 5 and the special-edition *Mission Commander Scout Squad Maximum Action Premiumized.*

Now the national hero was one of the Seats on the Motherboard—or Parentboard, as proposed equal-opportunity legislation would rename it. There were three seats in total: the Seat of Law, the Other Seat of Law and Yet Another Seat of Law. Nickelby was the Yet Another Seat, but he was the only one that mattered.

"When can I meet him? Will you introduce us?" Henry asked. "Does he know my name too?"

"Henry!" his mom barked, her voice modulator turned to I PROGRAMMED YOU BETTER THAN TO HOUND GUESTS AND SMALL PETS.

He mumbled sorry and sat on the couch in disgrace.

Erickson assured her he didn't mind. "A young bot should be enthusiastic. Now, regarding the assignment, I trust you'll accept knowing that the Motherboard is involved. Of course, if you absolutely cannot reverse your scruple programming, I will talk to the Motherboard on your behalf. I'm 87 percent certain the Seats won't demote you simply because you refused their hand-picked assignment."

Jacob's OddOdds placed the likelihood of no negative consequences at 1 in 10 and he sought out Jane's sight sensors before assuring his boss they would be delighted to take the ETC-420-GX-2 into their home. "But there will be ground rules," he said sharply at his son's excited whoop. "You *will* scan the manual from the first word to the last and follow the instructions to the letter. You'll use it only after you've finished your homework and your chores. At the first sign of berserkoness—and I mean the very first sign—you step away from it and get me or your mother. If you violate any of these rules, it goes to the compaction facility, no questions asked. Is that understood?"

"Yes, yes, yes," Henry said, happily agreeing to all the conditions. So what if he couldn't use it until all his chores were done? With the human doing his chores, they would be finished in no time. "Can we get it now? Please?"

His father glanced briefly at Jane, then nodded. Henry cheered again and charged out of the room. Within seconds, he was halfway down the driveway. His parents and Erickson followed at their normal pace, earning a grumble of disgust from Henry as they walked toward the curb. *Walking* at a time like this!

It was another forty-five and a half seconds before Erickson opened the trunk to reveal the brown cardboard box of the HueManTech ETC-420-GX-2.

After all these years, Henry Jacobson finally had his own human.

Yes!

HueManTech Human
Owner's Manual

UNIT CODE ETC-420-GX-2

MULTIFUNCTION CAPABILITY

Say hello to the newest member of your family, the HueManTech human multifunction Service with a Smile ETC-420-GX-2 unit! The ETC-420-GX-2 is a fully loaded, fully integrated, male-type ETC unit designed to perform a variety of functions within your home.

The ETC-420-GX-2 has new and improved patented Cerebral Cortextinator™ technology! New smart "logic board" makes "processing" a snap!

Please scan this manual thoroughly before use, and keep it where all those who use the product will upload it.

WARNINGS

! Human may become psychotic. If you see signs of deranged or berserko behavior, step away from the human and call 911 immediately.

! Do not disassemble. Touching the product's internal parts could result in injury. Repairs should be performed only by qualified technicians. Should the human break open as the result of a fall or other accident, take the product to a HueManTech-authorized service provider for inspection. Tampering with the product's internal parts could result in termination of warranty.

! Do not use in the presence of fire. Humans are highly flammable.

! Observe caution when handling. Humans may leak or explode if improperly handled. To prevent crying jags and fits of anger, treat with kindness.

PARTS OF THE HUMAN

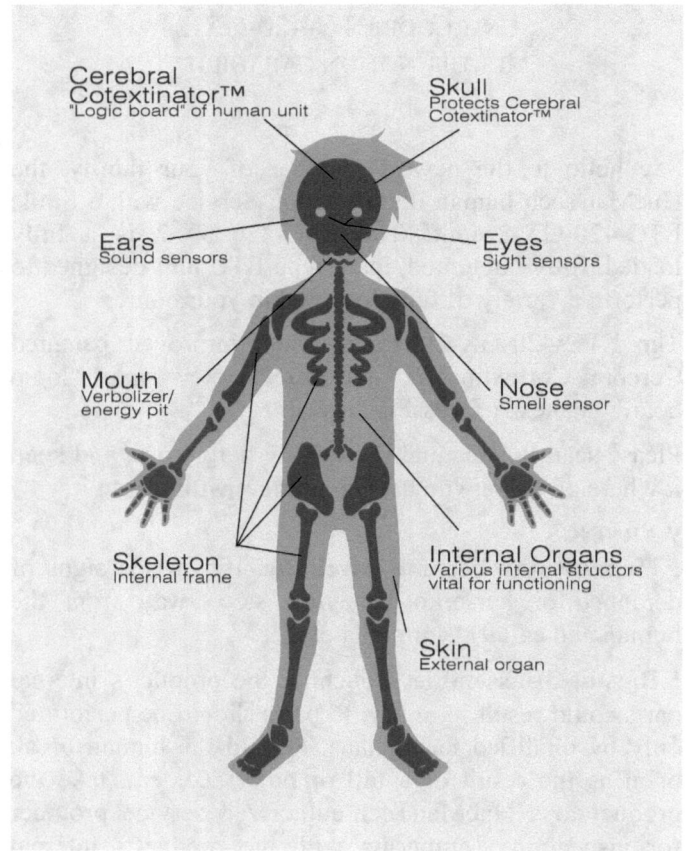

Skull: The hard outer shell that houses the Cerebral Cortextinator™, covered with hair. It can sustain repeated collisions with other hard objects but will swell at the point of impact. Apply cold pack (sold separately) to the bump and wait twenty-four hours. If unit behaves erratically, contact your service provider. Note: Some units may not have hair.

Cerebral Cortextinator™: The logic board of the human unit. It controls autonomic and cognitive functions. It runs smoothly on the proper amount of food and sleep. If worked too hard, it will develop a "headache," a condition in which the Cerebral Cortextinator™ aches from too much exertion. Let unit rest for eight hours before resuming normal function. If headache persists, contact your service provider.

Eyes: Sight sensors. The usefulness of a human's eyes is subject to the amount of light in its immediate vicinity. A human is unable to function in complete darkness. Eyes are sensitive to sunlight, and protective shields called SunGlasses™ are recommended (sold separately). Eyes may be defective in some units. Contact your HueManTech representative to arrange for a corrective laser repair operation (surcharge may apply).

Ears: Sound sensors. The ears can detect sounds with frequencies between 20 hertz and 20 kilohertz. They tend to fill with a sticky, yellow substance called ear "wax." Remove with a swab and resume normal function. Ears can be defective in some units. Contact your HueManTech representative to purchase a supplementary listening device. Ears also provide stability and balance.

Nose: Smell sensor. The nose is vital for respiration function, also called breathing, in which the human unit takes in and expels air. It is frequently filled with a slippery secretion known as mucous. Apply tissue (sold separately) to discharge. If mucous persists, contact your service provider for mucous tablets. The nose is also capable of detecting smells and aids the taste sensors.

Mouth: Verbalizor/energy pit. Also includes lips, tongue and teeth. The mouth is the main communication apparatus as well as the intake valve for food. It has four taste sensors: sweetness, bitterness, sourness and saltiness. Teeth require constant upkeep and brushing twice a day; a minty paste is highly recommended. (Toothbrush and paste sold separately.)

Internal organs: Include heart, lungs, stomach, liver, spleen and kidneys. A variety of internal structures provide a multitude of functions to keep your human unit running properly. Any one of these can malfunction at any time, usually accompanied by great pain. Wait until unit complains or doubles over in pain before contacting your service provider.

Skeleton: The internal frame of the human. It's constructed of loosely connected bones made of a frequently brittle calcium-phosphate alloy that can easily snap in two. Contact your service provider if you hear a crack. Apply daily doses of Calci-Yum!™ supplements to avoid breakage (sold separately).

Skin: The external organ of the human. The skin is covered with more than two dozen touch sensors at various points and comes in a range of colors. It is subject to a variety of conditions, including bruising, blistering and breakage. Repeated exposure to the sun can result in some units turning a bright red color. Remove from the sun and apply an aloe lotion (sold separately).

ACCESSORIES

Included in your purchase of your HueManTech ETC-420-GX-2 are the following. Contact your HueManTech dealer if any are missing.

* 1 storage container: A seven-by-seven-foot cardboard box. Also serves as your human's sleepstation. To assemble, fold the box along the dotted lines and place it in an unoccupied corner, preferably in a quiet portion of your home. This is your ETC-420-GX-2's "safe place" and where it will go to get "me-time." The optimum temperature for storing your unit is 72 degrees Fahrenheit.

* 6 all-purpose uniforms in a variety of HMT Action Colors: HueManTech's specially designed HMT Action Suit Jumpsuit provides your unit with all the clothing it needs for a week's worth of tasks. Rotate jumpsuits on a daily basis and clean once a week for maximum usage. Find more great styles and colors at HueManTech.com.

* 1 pair of all-terrain foot protectors in Splattered Mud: HueManTech's specially designed TreadMaster Shoes with Double-Thick Soles provide your unit with all the foot protection it needs for a year's worth of walking, running and tripping. With easy, zip-up enclosures any human can manage. Also available in Wet Soil and Tilled Ferrous.

 * 1 waste-treatment kit with 4 refills: HueManTech's patented two-step PoopPouf process gets rid of unsightly waste material. All units are programmed in the proper use of PoopPouf. Just supply your unit with a private corner in your backyard and forget about awkward biological functions forever. Refills available at HueManTech.com or at your local HueMart.

* 1 food starter kit: A one-week supply of Mega Additive Regular Function Energy Lastitive (MARFEL) meal pellets in four tasty flavors: sweet, bitter, sour and salty. Apply daily to keep your unit running smoothly. (Pellet serving amount based on the 2,000-calorie diet of a 150-pound human; individual needs may vary.) Refills available at HueManTech.com or at your local HueMart.

* 56 bottles of hydration fluid: A one-week supply of HueManTech's premeasured Go-Go Pep Solution, which uses HueManTech's special patented formula to create the maximum function-sustaining hydration fluid for your unit. Also included is a coupon for ten percent off your next purchase of 56 bottles. Refills available at HueManTech.com or at your local HueMart.

BASIC MAINTENANCE

Your HueManTech ETC-420-GX-2 needs to power down at night, just like you. It can't put itself into SLEEP mode, so it must be left in a dark, quiet place. Eventually, it will "fall" into SLEEP mode by accident. On average, humans require eight hours of sleep, but each unit varies slightly, and over time you will get to know your individual unit's needs. Try to put your ETC-420-GX-2 to sleep somewhere between nine and eleven P.M. for best results.

In addition to sleep, your ETC-420-GX-2 requires eight to twelve MARFEL meal-pellet meals a day to maintain its energy supply. You will know when your ETC-420-GX-2's energy is low when it responds slowly to commands and makes frequent errors. In extreme cases, your ETC-420-GX-2 might cease to work entirely and will simply lay its head down on a table. To restore normal function, apply two MARFEL meal pellets immediately and count to twenty.

It's also vital to keep your ETC-420-GX-2 well hydrated. Hydration fluid is necessary to its ability to function correctly. Apply eight-ounce doses of Go-Go Pep Solution at regular intervals.

Once your ETC-420-GX-2 has slept, eaten and downed a large bottle of hydration fluid, it's ready to go!

GETTING STARTED

Your HueManTech ETC-420-GX-2 responds to clear, explicit commands and works best when its owner provides detailed instructions. When ordering it to do a task, be as specific as possible. For example, don't say: Please clean the floor. Say: Please clean the living room floor with a mop dowsed in sudsy water from the mudroom. Precision is key to your ETC-420-GX-2's success.

Handle your ETC-420-GX-2 with care. It responds well to positive affirmation; apply a compliment when it does a task well. Always precede a command with *please* and follow with *thank you.* A little courtesy goes a long way in controlling your unit's emotionality.

Respect your ETC-420-GX-2's limitations. Don't ask it to perform tasks that are beyond its purview as listed in TASKS AND PURVIEW (section D, subset 83) or it will respond by growing frustrated, an extreme emotional state in which the human feels angry with itself but takes it out on everything around it. When it makes a mistake, patiently explain how to do the task correctly. A human's operating system isn't designed to integrate learned experience. However, it can recognize patterns if it performs an activity with enough frequency.

Learn to identify the signs of fatigue and hunger. Your ETC-420-GX-2 is prone to fits of emotionality when it needs sleep or to take in food. Also watch for signs of stress, a default setting in which your human's circuits are overworked and it can't compute basic commands. To repair, put your ETC-420-GX-2 in its storage container for an hour so it can have me-time in its safe place.

TROUBLESHOOTING

If your ETC-420-GX-2 fails to perform as expected, check the list of common problems below before consulting your service provider or certified HueManTech dealer. Note: Because each unit has individual variations in its programming, this list can provide only general guidelines. Keep in mind that your unit may display symptoms differently.

Problem: Your unit's eyes are watery and it releases puffs of air through its nose with a loud ahh-choo sound. **Likely cause:** Your unit has a "cold," a viral condition that affects its ability to process commands correctly because its Cortextinator aches.

Solution: Apply two HMT ColdAway tablets every four hours and let your unit sleep in its storage container. After twenty-four hours, your human unit should be as good as new.

Problem: Your unit's eyes are dripping and it emits a high-frequency whining sound from its mouth.

Likely cause: Your unit is depressed, an emotionality condition that can last anywhere from two minutes to twenty years.

Solution: Tell it a joke. Your human responds well to humor and likes to laugh. Find dozens of one-liners in HueManTech's best-selling books *Jokes to Cheer Up Your Human, More Jokes to Cheer Up Your Human* and *A Few More Jokes That We Left Out of Our Other Two Books to Cheer Up Your Human* at HueManTech.com.

Problem: Your unit's eyes stare into space and it expels air in long, extended puffs.

Likely cause: Your unit's "in love," an emotionality condition in which your human unit feels a strong attachment to another human unit.

Solution: Let the two units spend as much time together as possible. Love usually runs its course within a week.

HueManTech, HueManTech.com and the HueManTech logo are trademarks of HueManTech Corporation Inc.

CHAPTER FOUR
GO-GO PEP SOLUTION

By the time Henry finished uploading and scanning the HueManTech ETC-420-GX-2 instruction manual, his excitement at owning a new and improved Cerebral Cortextinator™ ETC unit was entirely gone. He couldn't believe that this flimsy gadget was the best on the market. New and improved—ha! It was old and inferior. According it its own instructions, it would probably spend more time in the shop than in the house.

Contact service provider. Contact service provider.

It said that on every single page.

Human cuts its finger? Contact service provider.

Human sneezes? Contact service provider.

Human impales itself on the backyard fence? Contact service provider.

Flickering flames, what was the *point*?

After making such a stink about the human, Henry thought it was probably best not to complain, but he wasn't very enthusiastic when his mom insisted on quizzing him on the basics. The manual was stored on one of his new drives, and she wasn't convinced it was working properly yet, especially since he failed his recent practical.

"What's a headache?" she asked, as she leaned against the capacitator, a Gorginaldo 10.58 in Energetic Yellow that had yet to be turned on. Despite promises of coal roasted in a pot, dinner had been put indefinitely on hold. His dad sat at the kitchen table opposite Henry, all 56 bottles of hydration fluid spread out before him.

"A malfunction caused by too much work," Henry said, looking over his mother's shoulder to where a lace curtain fluttered in the breeze. The kitchen was the least cluttered room in the house, with a row of blue cabinets over a slate counter and a coal capacitator that baked, broiled *and* burned. The cabinets were filled with coal—bags of fresh coal, boxes of prepulverized coal and cans of post-capacitated liquid coal for instant energy intake when you didn't have time to cook.

"How do you treat it?" Jane asked.

"Put it in SLEEP mode for eight hours."

"What do you do if the human is burned by the sun?"

"Apply an aloe treatment."

"When do you apply mucous tablets?"

"When the human has a cold."

His mom shook her head. "You apply ColdAway tablets when the human has a cold. Mucous tablets are for when the smell sensor secretes mucous."

Henry doubted there was any difference but he said, "Mucous tablets are for mucous. Check."

"How do you know when a human is psychotic?"

"It bashes you on the head with a mop," Henry said.

"Not all deranged humans have mops," his mom said.

Well, duh. He was just kidding. Who unscrewed his mom's funnybolt? His dad was just as bad. He was checking the safety caps on the bottles of hydration fluid to make sure that Henry wouldn't inadvertently splash himself with it as if he were a little botty. He could handle a few pints of liquid without frying himself.

"List three early indicators that a human might become psychotic," she said.

"Its eyes roll into its head. Its sentences become garbled." The first two came easily, but he couldn't access the third one from his memory bank because, to be completely honest, his new drive did get stuck sometimes. He replayed the scene from earlier today. The CRZ's sentences were certainly garbled. But what else? He had no idea. "It picks up a mop."

His parents still weren't amused.

"I think that's enough for tonight," Jacob said, looking up from the Go-Go Pep Solution bottle. "You still have some homework to do. We'll pick this up tomorrow when you're in a more productive mode."

"But I was just—"

"Your father is right. A human is not a toy, and when you understand the seriousness of the matter, we'll continue to review the manual. In the meantime, go to your room."

Henry stood up with a harrumph and grudgingly climbed the stairs. He didn't know what the big deal was. It wasn't like the human would be around that much anyway. It was going to spend most of its time in the repair shop. And yet his dad was already talking about ordering refills of the meal pellets.

There's the real joke, Henry thought. The human was just a way for HueManTech to sell junk to gullible customers. The human couldn't need *all* that stuff. It could probably get by on two jumpsuits. And what was with the waste-treatment kits? Did human units really create so much waste that it needed to be treated? Robots didn't create waste at all. Sometimes, and only *very* rarely, a bot would expel a small puff of black smoke from its fan region, but that only happened when coal wasn't made properly. To prepare it right, you had to cook the coal—roasting, frying, sautéing, boiling, baking, grilling and curing all worked—*before* pulverizing it. Then you liquefied it in a coal capacitator and poured it into your coal hole.

Henry entered his room and slammed the door, his emotionality stabilizer kicking in as the surge of anger shot through him. He knew the ability to control his feelings was just one of the million things that made him superior to the gadget down the hall. Humans were merely dumbed-down robots. He knew that. But he still expected more.

Even after the berserko human tried to demolish the Shine Bar with a mop, his expectations remained high. The salon's human was an old, outdated, off-the-shelf unit, probably on the cheap side. But the ETC-420-GX-2 was state-of-the-art. The Motherboard was even thinking about subsidizing it. It *had* to be something special.

But clearly one human was pretty much like another. Contact service provider.

Henry sat down at his studystation, a large, brown fixture as big as his dad's car. It was his bedroom, but he had no say over it. His mom picked out all the furniture. He'd wanted the Compacto Reduced Mini studystation, a single desk-and-drawer combo. But no, his mother insisted on the Deluxe Grand Superstar in Select Plus, which had twelve shelves, eight drawers, sixteen cubbyholes, a credenza, a hutch, a privacy hood and a disk receptacle. It was hulking and huge and left no room for a video game machine.

He knew that was part of his mom's plan. She wanted all video games to be confined to the living room, where she could keep a sight sensor on them.

Opposite the studystation was his bed, which was buried under a pile of swervy-striped pillows. A knitted sheet, a gift for his fourth upgrade, encased the mattress in hundreds of tiny helioballs. Next to it stood the cleansing closet, a small cabinet that dispensed quick-evaporating purification fluid (a 97.97 percent isopropyl solution) onto sparkle sponges. Every night, Henry wiped a moistened sponge over his frame to remove the grime of the day. He was supposed to do it in the morning, too, but he didn't see the point. How could he get dirty just lying in bed?

On the top shelf of the cabinet, a circus of knitted clownbots tumbled and jumped and swung from high bars. Henry knew the figurines were as bottyish as his helioball bedsheet, but he liked the red-smell-sensored juggler, who always seemed on the verge of dropping the five rainbow-colored balls that somehow remained in the air.

Henry initialized his essay-writing app to begin his homework, which was to make an argument for or against the Use Chain.

The Use Chain described the machine hierarchy on Ferrous. Machines at the top of the evolutionary ladder, such as robots, were free to use the machines below them on the ladder in any manner they saw fit. Consolis, for example, a dependent mineralizer that grew in open fields, was harvested, treated and loaded with software to be used as video game consoles. Sedanmobiles, which roamed the Vast Open Space of the Very Far West, were caught and domesticated to be used as cars like his dad's Esperzo or his mom's Ergmenty.

Some robots argued that it was wrong for any machine, including robots, to use another machine. They believed all sedanmobiles should be set free and all consolis left alone to grow wild. They were even against the domestication of small machines as household pets, even though those machines were protected and treated kindly.

Anti-Use-Chainers argued that the invention of human technology made the need for machine exploitation unnecessary, since humans were created specifically to do the jobs robots didn't want to do. If humans could fulfill a function, then there was no reason for robots to exploit their fellow machines on Ferrous.

Henry thought there were many flaws in this reasoning. For one, humans were good for only some things such as mining coal for food or operating an elevator. But they'd never be as efficient as a calculator. For another, there were some things they simply couldn't do like fly. Sure,

HueManTech promised every year to produce a flying model but one had yet to appear. Lastly, no matter how advanced the technology got, you still could never play *Mission Commander Scout Squad* on a human unit because they didn't have screens.

Although he knew he had a strong argument, Henry was too distracted by the ETC-420-GX-2 down the hall to make it. There was a human in his house. For the first time ever. How was he supposed to concentrate?

Maybe if he saw the unit and operated it for a few minutes, his curiosity would be appeased and he'd be able to finish his homework. His parents wouldn't object. They wanted him to get good grades. (Remember the goal, Henry!) Besides, they were too engrossed by PoopPouf pills and the various ways you could identify a berserko human to even notice.

Quietly, Henry crept down the hall to the back room, which housed the ETC-420-GX-2's quiet corner. This was his mom's hobby room. All robots had a relaxation protocol. Sports, scanning, shopping, doodling—there were hundreds of options. Jane's was knitting, and she did it at a dizzying pace, churning out more fannypacks, pillows and figurines than anybot needed. She'd even knitted wallpaper for the room itself—purple and blue tree formations against a yellow sky.

His dad's hobby was model shipbuilding, but he hadn't initiated his app since the day he was promoted to department head.

The human, contrary to its own owner's manual, was not in its storage container, which Henry's dad had immediately assembled, per the instructions. Instead, it was lying on *top* of the box, which it had flattened and folded over.

Henry wasn't surprised the human lacked the cognitive function to know that it was supposed to sleep *inside* the box. He just thought it was a good sign that the unit wasn't sleeping *under* it. The ETC-420-GX-2 had also taken one of its six jumpsuits and rolled it into a ball that it stuck under its head.

Curious, Henry bent down to get a closer look at the

human unit, which was lying on its back. He'd never been this close to one before and was surprised by how colorful it was: peach skin, pink cheeks, yellow hair, red lips, brown freckles. Its skin apparatus was smooth but unreflective and had none of the wrinkles and spots that the spa's human had. It was also shorter and more compact than other humans and had a speculative chronological age of thirteen upgrades—which was unusual since the average SCA of a human unit was twenty-five to forty-five. Like Henry, the ETC-420-GX-2 was five feet, two inches tall. Henry knew he would grow another twelve inches like his dad; he had no data on whether humans also attained additional height.

Leaning in closer, he detected the sound of air moving in and out of its mouth. At first he was confused but then he realized the noise was respiration. The human was breathing.

Fascinated despite himself, he lifted a hand to touch it. The Shine Bar's Drudgery unit's skin had been rough like concrete, but the ETC-420-GX-2's looked soft. Would it feel different? Henry ran his touch sensor lightly along the arm that peeked out from under the orange jumpsuit. It was warm and dotted with a few almost invisible hairs.

Henry wondered what purpose they served.

He knew very little about human technology. Like every school kid, he knew that Dr. Felix J. Tinsmith invented the appliance forty years ago. He knew that Tinsmith's discovery of the cerebral cortextinator made speech and movement possible. But he didn't understand how a human worked. A robot was an algorithm-based life form that ran on an electrical charge maintained by a steady supply of energy. Humans, by contrast, pooped and ate pellets and frequently broke down.

Contact service provider.

And yet Henry couldn't look away from this human and he couldn't stop touching it. He moved his hand to its face to feel the skin there.

Suddenly, the human opened its eyes.

They were blue.

CHAPTER FIVE

CONTACT SERVICE PROVIDER

The last thing Henry expected to see were blue eyes—and not just any blue but the deep, bright blue of the afternoon sky. He thought all humans had muddy-brown eyes like the Drudgery at the spa.

The ETC-420-GX-2 blinked at Henry and sat up. "Hey there," it said, opening its mouth wide and expelling air. Its eyes shuttered closed for a split second.

Henry knew the blinking was normal. Like breathing, humans did many strange things. They were called technical innovations and were vital to the appliance's ability to function.

The "hay there," however, was odd because there weren't any stalks of marcasite hay there or anywhere in the room. Henry started to point that out, then stopped. The owner's manual didn't say anything about correcting your unit in the course of regular conversation. This wasn't a task, so there wasn't an opportunity to learn. Not that the ETC-420-GX-2 could learn much anyway.

In the end, Henry decided to teach by example. "Hello," he said, hoping the human would get the point. But he knew it probably wouldn't.

Giving no indication either way, the ETC-420-GX-2 stretched its arms over its head and exhaled again. "Hey, it's good to be awake." Henry realized then that the repeated use of "hay" was a glitch in the ETC-420-GX-2's programming. He wondered if he should contact his service provider. "I feel like I've been asleep for years. But I'm ready for my tour of the house. Can we start in the kitchen? I'm starving."

As he talked, the human unrolled the jumpsuit, folded it neatly and added it to the pile of other jumpsuits. Henry was happy to see the ETC-420-GX-2 could follow simple cleaning protocols. He decided to give it its first command. "Please reassemble your storage container by unfolding the box and refolding it along the dotted lines to create a safe place for you to spend your me-time."

The human smiled and looked down at the box it was standing on, but didn't jump to follow the order. If anything, it seemed confused.

Recalling the operating manual, Henry reissued the command with more detail. "Please reassemble your storage container by stepping off the box and bending down to grab one end of it with your hands. Pull that end until the box is lying flat. Then use your hands to refold the box along the dotted lines and lift the sides to create an open space in the middle."

The ETC-420-GX-2 laughed. "Hey, *yo comprendo*, bro. I was just trying to get the point."

Henry's wires buzzed softly as his language app identified the language, Near Northern, and his geography app attributed it to another land mass. Henry lived on the Central Land Mass, which consisted of three countries: the United Territories, the Extreme South and the Very Far West.

While Henry puzzled over the strangeness of the human unit knowing Near Northern, his language app translated the foreign phrase. *I understand.*

No, you don't, Henry thought, frustration starting to work its way through his emotionality stabilizer. Clearly this human was as dumb as the spa's unit. Or maybe dumber. At least the one at the Shine Bar knew how to use its own storage container. *And* it didn't have a persistent malfunction that made it say *hay* before every sentence.

The ETC-420-GX-2 was *clearly* a reject.

Patiently, per the manual, Henry explained the use of the storage container as a place for the human to fall into SLEEP mode. The ETC-420-GX-2 nodded. "It's not that I don't want a place to"—here it raised two fingers on each hand and bent them as it spoke—"'fall into SLEEP mode' but I'd rather not do it in a box. It's not like I've got claustrophobia or anything, but the air gets hot and stale pretty darn quick in a space that small. Plus, the floor is hard, so the extra padding helps."

Henry's wires hummed with increased activity as he searched his database for the word *claustrophobia.* His dictionary came up blank, as did his language app. Assuming this was an error, he tried again.

Nope, nothing.

"*Claustrophobia* does not compute," he said.

"I'm not surprised," it said. "I made it up. From the Very Far Western word *claustrum* meaning 'a bolt, place shut in' and the Extreme Southern word *phobia* meaning 'fear.' So *claustrophobia* means 'fear of small places.' Which I don't have. But nor do I want to sleep in an airless cardboard box. But, hey, I'm only human."

Now Henry's wires whirred loudly as he struggled to process all the information conveyed by the ETC-420-GX-2. A human not wanting to sleep *in its own* storage container because the air was *hot and stale*? Huh? Humans didn't have preference settings. They did what they were told to do. What did it mean that the floor was hard? It didn't have enough touch sensors to register hard or soft. And how about the way it failed to follow an order? Henry had given it a *specific* command, and the ETC-420-GX-2 ignored it completely because it didn't make sense to it. Humans weren't capable of advance functions like making sense. *Nothing* made sense to them. Oh, and *making up words*? Humans were lucky enough to be able to put two words together at all. But creating *new* ones with other *languages* from faraway places that the human can't possibly have heard of?! That was pure insanity.

His fan kicked in.

Absolute insanity.

Total derangement.

Suddenly, Henry felt his hazard meter activate. The ETC-420-GX-2 didn't seem berserko in the mop-wielding, nonsense-chanting kind of way, but what if making up words was the early-warning sign he couldn't remember?

The CRZ78BX-22 had spouted nonsense during its berserko fit, and what was the word *claustrophobia* if not pure nonsense?

The ETC-420-GX-2 was careening toward crazy. All it needed was a mop and a mirror to smash.

Slowly, Henry backed out of the room. He didn't want to surprise the unit with any sudden movements. "All right," he said, his voice modulator turned to AS SOOTHING AS A CRACKLING FIRE as he closed the door, "you don't have to sleep in the small, airless box. Sleep wherever you like. Whatever makes you happy."

He could see the ETC-420-GX-2 smile through the crack. "Cool, bro. You're the best," it said, the last few words muffled by the door. "But what about my pellets?"

In the hallway, Henry lost no time. He dashed down the stairs, jumping over the last two, and ran through the living room. He knew he'd get lectured for disobeying a command—maybe even punished—but it was much more important that they know about the deranged human in their house. That thing could have short-circuited them all in the middle of the night! The thought was terrifying. He and his mom had already been harrowed by one berserko human that day. What were the odds that they'd be harrowed by a second?

His OddOdds probability app ran the numbers (1 in 690,642) as Henry burst into the kitchen and told his parents to contact their service provider.

CHAPTER SIX
PERFECTLY NORMAL STIMULI

Henry's parents made him go to school the next day.

"But we can't leave it alone in the house," he said, his voice modulator turned to HAS AN AIRCOPTER CRUSHED YOUR LOGIC BOARD?

"It'll be fine by itself," his mom insisted as she added another item to the list of things she had to do to get the Shine Bar back in shape. "Human units are designed to spend time alone."

"That's not what I meant," Henry said, exasperated. He'd spent one hour, twelve minutes and eleven seconds last night trying to convince his folks that the ETC-420-GX-2 was berserko, but they insisted its behavior fell within normal parameters. "It's too dangerous to leave on its own. It might burn down the house or kill the neighbors."

Jane smiled. "Humans don't have the ability to make fire and all the neighbors work during the day."

Henry didn't appreciate the joke. Berserkoness was no laughing matter. Obviously his mom was too overwhelmed by the monumental task of putting her spa back together to think clearly. "Dad," he said.

Jacob zipped his fannypack closed. "I understand your concern, son, and I commend you for it. You should always be wary of the unfamiliar. However, in this case, your hazard meter is merely being overly cautious. After your experience with the demented human yesterday, it's registering everything as a potential risk. It's a common response. Eventually your hazard meter will settle down and start filtering out perfectly normal stimuli again."

Henry felt like his circuits were frying. No matter what the evidence, his parents dismissed it as perfectly normal. He'd shown them the flattened storage container and the fluffed jumpsuit-pillow. He'd relayed the claustrophobia conversation.

Did they care?

No.

They weren't even worried that it knew foreign languages like Very Far Western, Extreme Southern or Near Northern. "Manufacturer's defect," his dad had insisted. "HueManTech must have loaded it with those languages by mistake."

His mom had been equally blasé. "In refolding that jumpsuit, the ETC-420-GX-2 has already done more cleaning than the CRZ78BX-22."

The only thing they'd conceded was strange was the way it started every sentence with the word *hay*. But his dad shrugged and said, "Harmless quirk."

Henry couldn't believe his parents were so obtuse. And now they wanted to leave this storage-container-flattening, jumpsuit-fluffing, Extreme Southern– and Very Far Western–speaking, *hay*-spouting malfunctioning appliance alone in their home. It did not compute.

He tried his mom again. "But you *said* it would go

back at the first sign of trouble. It's already causing problems. I didn't finish my homework last night because I was too busy worrying about the demented human down the hall killing me in my sleep."

Jane added another item to her list, then looked up. "Henry, darling, humans are increasingly part of our lives. You should embrace the technology, not fear it. It was my mistake not to realize that sooner, and I apologize. Now get your backpack and I'll drop you at school on my way to work."

School was awful.

Word of the CRZ78BX-22's berserkoness had spread quickly, and everyone thought it was hilarious that his mother had taken it down while Henry watched helplessly.

"Poor little Lanky Hanky had to be saved by his mommy-wommy," Evan Leadfoot called out while Sissy decided whom to pick next for her helioball team.

They were in gym class; otherwise, Henry wouldn't have been within ten feet of a helioball court. He stunk at the game. All the running, jumping, sweeping, spinning and throwing required too many of his apps to be open at once. As soon as the ball landed in his grasp, his entire team would shout at him—where to throw it, whom to throw it to—and the pressure inevitably led to a crash. Now, instead of even trying to catch the ball, he ran in the other direction.

For this reason, he was always last to be picked.

Today, however, Johnny, who everyone called Negative Point One because his microchip processed data so slowly, it practically moved backward, was playing. The two of them were the only ones left.

As Sissy ran Henry's and Johnny's stats through her skill-tabulating app to help her decide which player to choose, Henry wished he could disappear. The modern robot had more than twenty thousand apps, and yet not a single one could make you invisible. Why hadn't that been invented years before? It would certainly be more useful than stupid humans.

Thinking of the uselessness of humans reminded him yet again—though, really, how could he forget—that the ETC-420-GX-2 was alone in his house causing untold destruction. It was probably going through his things right now, planting little booby traps in his drawers and tearing up his MegaBot comics.

The skill-tabulating app beeped, and Sissy scanned the results, then looked up at the gym instructor. "It came up a draw. Do I really have to pick one?"

The teacher told her she did. "And you have to put him in the game. No sticking him on the bench like last time."

Sissy grumbled but chose Henry.

"Aw," groaned Evan, who had been picked during the first round.

Henry kept his sight sensors down as Sissy assigned positions. To no one's surprise, he got backward guard, the player who stood behind the net facing away from the field to catch the ball before it dropped out of bounds.

Helioball was a simple game: Shoot the helioball into the opposing team's basket as many times as possible during two 21-minute halves. The trick was making the basket while the ball was on fire. Blazing nets were worth four points. Unblazing nets were worth one. Running and bouncing the ball was fine as long as it wasn't on fire; as soon as it burst into flames, you had to throw it. Holding on to a flaming ball resulted in hazards, penalties and a one-point deduction for every half second you held the ball.

Since backward guard got little action, Henry spent most of his time on the field trying to process his parents' inexplicable reaction. How could they not be the least bit concerned? They, who had always been so vehemently opposed to human technology that they were practically honorary members of the Robothood of Peace? All his life, they had gone on about how unreliable and destructive humans were. Then one enters their house *speaking Very Far Western* and sleeping *on top of* its box, and they welcome it like a lost member of the family.

It did not compute.

Their reality affirmulators had to be on the fritz, Henry thought. It was the only explanation that made sense. The reality affirmulator objectively appraised situations and confirmed that they were real. When it stopped working, a robot couldn't tell fact from fiction, a condition called bent-reality syndrome.

Clearly, his parents had it and they had it bad.

The question was, how to fix it? His parents would never agree to run a self-diagnostic. If you knew your reality was off, then your reality wasn't off. That was bent syndrome 101. No, he would have to somehow trick them into checking into the Rutherford Institution for Reality Disorders. But the question was—

"Get it, get it, get it," Sissy suddenly shouted.

Henry looked up. The helioball was hurtling toward him. Immediately, he opened his vector app to judge the angle, his length app to measure the distance and his velocity app to calculate speed. Thirty-three feet. Twenty-nine feet. Twenty-two feet.

It grew closer and closer.

Next to him, Sissy yelled, "Get it! Get it! Get it!"

Across from her, Evan made a botty face. "Does little Lanky Hanky need helpy-welpy?"

Fifteen feet. Eight feet. Two feet.

He caught it just as the ball ignited.

"Throw it! throw it! throw it!" Sissy screamed.

"He needs his mommy to throw it for him," Evan jeered.

Seconds ticked by. Two points gone. Four points gone. Six points gone.

Henry looked at the court, his sight sensors struggling to focus on a player. Chrissy was open. Wait. No, she wasn't. George was blocking her. Tony. No, Priscilla. Yes, Priscilla was free.

All he had to do was throw it to her.

Eight points gone. Ten points gone.

His vector app gauged the angle. His length app measured the distance. He opened his force app to calculate the amount of power to apply to the ball.

The *wzzz* was immediate and insistent.

Sissy grew shrill.

Evan grew meaner.

The sound grew louder.

Fourteen points gone. Sixteen points gone.

Wzzz. Wzzz. Wzzz.

The world went black.

CHAPTER SEVEN
MEANING "TO STUN WITH A POLE AND AN AX"

While the ETC-420-GX-2 wiped, washed, scrubbed, scraped, rubbed, rinsed, dusted and disinfected every inch of the Jacobsons' house, Henry kept watch. When it scooched under the couch to clear out three years of dust, Henry scooched under it too. When it braved the deep reaches of the hall closet, Henry braved them too.

The human unit didn't seem to mind. Henry expected it to snap or complain, but all it did was smile like it was happy to have the company. Sometimes, it asked Henry to pass the bucket or a sponge.

Henry wasn't fooled. He knew the human was on the brink of a giant malfunction. Everything it did proved it. This morning, it asked his mom if she'd slept well. That was a huge indicator. Humans weren't loaded with etiquette protocols, nor were they programmed for small talk.

Something awful was about to happen, and only Henry could prevent it. His parents were no help. They had been *completely* taken in. Last night, his dad had given it a screwdriver—aka deadly weapon that could scrape out his logic board—so it could fix the rickety back door. "If I had known how handy this little human gadget was, I'd have gotten one years ago," Jacob said, inspecting the hinges.

And now his mom had provided it with unlimited access to all the murderous mops and brooms it could possibly want. We're all goners, Henry thought as he followed the ETC-420-GX-2 to the shed, where it fetched the lawnshaver. The human appeared to be harmlessly going about its business, but Henry knew it was up to something nefarious.

He still couldn't believe his parents had left him alone with the unit. Usually on Saturday they dragged him to the mall to look at fabric swatches or whatever boring errand they were running. But today they wanted him to rest because of yesterday's crash. Jane even suggested she stay with him, but Henry begged her not to. It would be unbearable if anyone from school found out his mom had to stay home with him. He could just hear Evan's smart comment about little Lanky Hanky needing a botty-sitter.

Yesterday was bad enough. When his mother came to pick him up from the nursestation at school, she insisted they stop in his classroom to get his homework assignment. Mrs. Yitteriumski eagerly congratulated her on capably handling the berserko human. She even led the class in a round of applause.

Twenty-one hours, sixteen minutes and thirty-eight seconds later, he still wished he could delete the moment from his memory bank.

The human switched the shaver out of SLEEP mode and began shaving. "You can watch me from inside too," it said suddenly.

Henry's hazard meter hummed. The human was initiating conversation, another behavior outside its parameters. It was only supposed to *respond* to commands. The comment itself contributed to the MAYBE HAZARDOUS rating. *Why* did it want Henry to go inside? What would it do when he did?

Henry remained exactly where he was.

The ETC-420-GX-2 started at the edge of the lawn, near the trim of dusk-blooming nightlights. "Hey, it's cool if you want to hang with me. I like the company. But I know your parents wanted you to rest and hanging with me isn't resting. Plus, the sun is hot. That can't be good for your system. Inside you've got cool shade, cushy chairs and a perfect view of me and my many labors. It's the trifecta of comfort."

Oh, great, Henry thought. Now the *human* was treating him like a botty. He could not think of anything more humiliating. "I don't need to rest," he snapped. "I feel fine, so I don't need your trifecta of comfort. *Trifecta* isn't even a word."

"It is now," the ETC-420-GX-2 said with a grin. "It means to achieve a group of three things. From the Near Eastern *tres* meaning 'three' and the Extreme Southern *perfecta* meaning 'perfect.'"

Henry felt his wires begin to sizzle—and not from the heat of the sun. The ETC-420-GX-2 was clearly unbalanced. It didn't follow any protocols at all. When a robot stopped following its protocol, you knew it had a permanent error. From there it was a short jump to total shutdown.

But this human unit did whatever it wanted whenever it wanted with no repercussions. Henry knew it was only a stupid gadget, but the fact that it got away with stuff bugged him.

"You can't make up new words," Henry said.

The human stopped, examined its handiwork and started a new row. "I like making up new words. Don't you?"

"Robots don't make up words. *Everyone* knows that."

The ETC-420-GX-2 blinked its eyes a few times. "Huh. Where do words come from then?" it asked, sounding genuinely confused.

"From the dictionary app's database," Henry said as if talking to a first-upgrader. "Everyone has it installed in their second, eighth, twelfth and sixteenth upgrades."

"Yeah, but where do those words come from?"

Henry initialized his verbalizor to give the obvious answer but then realized there wasn't an obvious answer.

He didn't know where the words in the database came from. Immediately, he scanned the app's help section, which explained how to interpret individual entries but didn't say anything about the words' origins.

Uncertain, Henry processed the question. If the dictionary didn't have the answer, he'd have to find it somewhere else. He pulled up A *Short Compendium of Robotivity* and keyword-searched for *language* and *word invention.* Nothing.

All right, he thought unconcernedly. If he couldn't find the answer, he would compute it. But the longer he processed the question, the more logical the ETC-420-GX-2's assumption seemed. Words had to come from some place. They didn't just fall from the sky arranged alphabetically in a dictionary program. (The reasonator had spit out that hypothesis before Henry had even finished forming it.) So they had to originate from intelligent life.

The only intelligent life on the planet was robot.

But that meant the human was right. A microchipless gadget was *right,* and he, a superior robot being, the top machine on the evolutionary ladder, was *wrong.*

Henry's OddOdds buzzed, then spurted, as it tried to calculate the likelihood of that: 1 in 49,322. No, 1 in 811,630. No, 1 in 6,494,228,002.

The numbers grew higher and higher at a dizzying rate, the algorithm spiraling out of control as Henry tried to process the seemingly unprocessable idea that humans were smarter *and* dumber than robots.

His reasonator grappled with the data, whirring as it struggled to make sense of it. Henry felt the buzzing through his entire frame and heard the familiar *wzzz-wzzz.* Afraid he was about to collapse on the lawn in front of all the neighbors, leaving himself vulnerable to public humiliation and whatever dastardly plan the human was hatching, he closed his dictionary app, his textbook-reading app and his odds-making app. The *wzzz-wzzz* faded, and an error message popped up: No. 429.

Henry had no idea what error 429 was. At school, they'd covered only messages 1 through 275. He searched his message-defining app for an explanation. 304: syllogism. 361: sedoku. 406: foreign object in processor.

Then he found it. 429: irreconcilable paradox.

Recommended handling: Concede one assumption is wrong.

Which assumption?

His processor hummed as he considered the contradictory halves of the paradox. He couldn't concede humans were smarter. Their stupidity was established fact and not up for debate. But he also couldn't concede that humans were dumber because in this case the human was right and the robot was wrong.

Maybe that was the solution. In some rare cases—some very, *very* rare cases that happened once every four million years—a human was smarter than a robot. But not all the way smarter. Just about one thing.

Like where words came from.

"Hey, hey," the ETC-420-GX-2 said, waving his hand in front of Henry. "Hey, are you OK in there?"

As the error message cleared up, Henry's sight sensors registered the concern on the ETC-420-GX-2's face. "I'm fine, thanks," he said.

"Man, you looked totally poleaxed," it said.

His dictionary turned up nothing on *poleaxed*. Not surprised, Henry searched *pole* and *ax* and combined the two definitions. "Meaning 'to stun with a pole and an ax,'" he said. "From the Near Northern *palus* meaning 'stake' and the Middle Eastern *ackus* meaning 'a cutting tool that consists of a heavy-edged head fixed to a handle.'"

The human clapped. "Exactly. Now you go."

At first Henry didn't know what it meant. He wasn't going to go and leave the human alone on the front lawn. But then he realized the ETC-420-GX-2 meant it was his turn to make up a word.

Henry didn't want to play the stupid game, but he couldn't accept the idea that the human might be better than he at something. So he gave it a try, methodically pairing words in his dictionary. The game wasn't as easy as it seemed. You couldn't simply combine any old two words and expect the new one to make sense.

He needed a different approach and initialized a search of all his applications to find the one that would apply to the situation. Not his textbook reader. Not his way finder. Not his skills tabulator.

None of his programs seemed right.

I need another method, he realized. How did the human do it? It described an experience or feeling.

Henry look around him for something to describe. He saw the lawn, nightlights, the street, their neighbor Mrs. Zincfield.

Nothing.

Time passed.

The ETC-420-GX-2 didn't seem to notice how long it was taking, but Henry knew. Every passing second was humiliating. He was supposed to be stronger, faster, better.

The sun beat down on his head.

The sun!

"Sunstruck," he said excitedly, "meaning 'to be hit with the sun.' From the Near Eastern *solaris* meaning 'sun' and the Distant Northern *strican* meaning 'to stroke.'"

"Hey, great one," it said with a big grin.

The wave of sheer delight Henry felt at the compliment was instantly downgraded to mild pleasure, but the charge of it lingered in his circuits and he found himself grinning back. In the sunlight, the human's sight sensors sparkled with as much light as Sissy O'Thalium's, and seeing it, Henry suddenly felt unsettled. He knew the hint of awareness he'd caught in the ETC-420-GX-2's eyes was just a trick of the bright sun. The human didn't actually think or reasonate.

But there was something unquestionably unusual about this unit, and Henry knew that was a problem. Humans were mass-produced in factories to be standardized, and variations on the standard never ended well. The CRZ78BX-22 was proof of that.

And then there was its enthusiastic approval, which, for a flash, had meant more to him than any endorsement from his parents or teachbots. That was a problem too.

Without saying a word, Henry left the ETC-420-GX-2 alone on the front lawn and went up to his room to run a diagnostic.

CHAPTER EIGHT
T COZIES—WHAT AND WHY?

All six diagnostics Henry ran on his operating system during the weekend came back normal. The numbers on his reaction times were on the high side, but the sluggish response was probably the result of the recent upgrade. Integration always slowed the processor down.

Even though the data emphatically proved that everything was all right, Henry still felt uneasy. He *knew* what he saw in the human's eyes—it was awareness. There for only the briefest of moments, it flickered as brightly as any sun. But Henry also knew that was impossible. The human was a mass-produced gadget designed to make life easier. It was a thing. Awareness couldn't possibly have flashed from the artificial sight sensors of a *thing*.

The only explanation that made sense to Henry was a malfunction in *his* reality affirmulator caused by the recent upgrade. But the very fact that he was willing to consider his reality was off meant his reality *wasn't* off.

No, the problem wasn't with him. It was with the ETC-420-GX-2. OK, so maybe the human wasn't about to tear out his logic board and pound it into a million little bytes. But there was definitely something different about the unit. No matter what Mr. Erickson said about it being a regular generalist model undergoing average-family evaluation, the ETC-420-GX-2 wasn't regular. It could do things no other human could.

Like be aware.

Knowing that made Henry feel unsettled, as if some of his wires had been cut.

For this reason, he decided to stay in his room for the rest of the day and get a jump on his homework, which wasn't due until Wednesday. He had to write a 1,000-word essay on the robot living or dead whom he admired most.

That was easy: Mission Commander Herbert Nickelby, winner of the Vanadiumian Metal of Distinction and greatest robot in the history of the world.

One: He co-invented the human with Dr. Felix J. Tinsmith. Tinsmith was the official technologist on the project, but everybot knew that it was Nickelby who kept him focused on the project when all his efforts seemed to fail. Tinsmith died of a massive binary infarction three months before the unit hit stores, so Nickelby named the debut model, the Smith 100-X-1, after him as a tribute.

Two: He single-handedly brought down the Robothood of Peace, the anti-technology cyberterrosim group that masterminded the ZombieBombie attack on HueManTech that shut down the corporation's entire system for three weeks. He infiltrated the organization by having his logic board implanted into another frame, an operation so dangerous it hadn't been performed before or since.

Three: He created the best video game ever: *Mission*

Commander Scout Squad. You could score five zillion and twenty-seven points and *still* not reach the highest level.

Four: He introduced lots of important legislation as Yet Another Seat of Law. Henry didn't actually know any law in particular that Nickelby had introduced, but he was sure there were dozens of ones vital to the safety and security of all Vanadiumians.

Far from being impressed or comforted by their son's unprecedented industriousness, his parents feared it was a sure sign of system malfunction. Ordinarily, Henry put off his assignments until the night before, when his mom would turn off the video game and send him to his studystation to do his homework. The fact that he was voluntarily getting a jump on the week convinced them his system was more affected by the crash than their diagnostics indicated. As a result, they kept ducking their heads into the room to make sure he was still running.

Nothing he said convinced them he was all right.

When a knock sounded on the door for the fifth time, Henry felt strong impatience wind its way through his emotionality stabilizer. It emerged as slight annoyance. "I'm fine," he called.

He didn't turn around or say come in, but of course his mom opened the door.

"Really, I'm fine," he repeated, swiveling around in his chair to find the ETC-420-GX-2 standing on the threshold, not his mom.

And there, Henry realized, discomfort shooting through his circuits, was the entire problem summed up. The human should never have known to open the door without being *told* to do so.

The ETC-420-GX-2 had abilities beyond anything he had ever seen.

"Good to know," it said with a grin.

The grin didn't help. Other humans walked around with their tongues hanging out and drool dripping down their chins. This one kept its mouth closed.

And what did it have to be so happy about anyway? It was an *appliance* designed to do boring household chores, carrying out an existence of preprogrammed servitude.

Processing it, Henry realized the lack of rationality in the ETC-420-GX-2's completely inappropriate emotional response to its miserable situation was the first sign of unintelligence he had seen in the human.

It made him feel better.

Henry turned back around.

"Hey, do you have a sec?"

Henry didn't answer. He didn't have to. A human was not owed basic courtesy.

"I've got some points that need clarification."

Henry continued to work on his essay.

"Hey, it's cool if you've got too much going on but it's really just a few Qs," the human said. "Nothing big."

Henry couldn't believe it was still there. He leaned forward and lowered the volume on his sound sensors to QUIET AS A CALCULATOR.

"What are T cozies and why would I want to crochet one?"

If the ETC-420-GX-2 had suddenly grown wings and flown away, Henry couldn't have been more surprised. T was short for treated coal, a heated sludge drink made from precapacitated coal that his mom's clients at the Shine Bar liked to pour down their energy pits. A cozy kept it hot.

Henry spun around. "What?"

"T cozies. What and why?"

Henry was speechless. His reasonator buzzed with data but no conclusions emerged. T cozies? Crocheting? Huh?

"OK, let's start with an easier one," the ETC-420-GX-2 said. "Midcentury cluttered. Is it right for me?"

It's finally lost it, Henry thought. Any second now it was going to start waving a mop. There was no other explanation for such random questions.

Then he noticed the glossy magazine in its hand. Glossies were another innovation of the new paper technology, which had been invented as a way to communicate with humans, who couldn't upload data. Some robots still preferred the outdated monthly download, but most enjoyed the novel, extremely satisfying tactile experience of holding something in their hands. Plus, paper didn't leave a traceable electrode trail, so you could scan whatever you wanted without anyone else knowing it.

"What is that?" Henry asked, nodding toward the glossy.

The human held it up. *"Good Roboting: For the Modern Robot."*

"For the middle-aged robot," Henry muttered. "That's my mom's mag. Why are you scanning it?"

It shrugged. "Nothing else to do."

"Well, it's boring. Here"—Henry grabbed *MegaBot #245: MegaBot Versus the Swamp Monster* and tossed it—"scan this. It's much more interesting. I have a bunch more when you finish that one."

The human immediately opened to page one and smiled at the brightly colored drawings. "Supercool. Thanks."

"No problem," Henry said.

The ETC-420-GX-2 thanked him again and wandered off to its storage container to read the comic book. Henry watched it go, then returned to his homework assignment. He was halfway through the conclusion when the true shocker of the conversation struck him: The human could scan. Sure, most humans could recognize a few words and decipher pictures, but the ETC-420-GX-2 could read whole *paragraphs* and *process* their meaning.

With that realization, he felt more unsettled than ever.

The Shine Bar Spa & Boutique's
meet our

super new human
sale

Get a free **buff** with any of our exclusive
Shine Services, including **waxing,
realignment, tinting** and **massage**

PLUS:
Save **20%** off all
aromatherapy candles and
essential oils!

One Day Only!

Extended!!!

The Shine Bar Spa & Boutique
"Because Beauty Is Blinding"

478 Disk Drive
Sodium Falls, NA11
866-SHINE-ME

CHAPTER NINE
MEGABOT VERSUS THE MEDUSA MONSTER

No one warned Henry about the sign.

That was all he could think as he opened the door to the Shine Bar for his after-school shift and spotted his mom across the floor talking to a customer. No one had even told him that the ETC was working in the salon.

The salon was remarkably full for a Wednesday afternoon—or any afternoon. It didn't even draw this large a crowd on Saturdays. There were so many clients milling around that the staff lounge had been turned into another waiting room.

Henry was amazed.

It couldn't be because of the human unit.

Could it?

"Oh, good, you're here," Jane said, sliding behind the reception station to consult the schedule. "There's a new delivery of tintelage in the storeroom in desperate need of unpacking. Can you handle it?"

She didn't bother to wait for an answer so Henry didn't get a chance to say, No, I can't handle it. Unpacking boxes was chip-numbing human work.

Henry expected to find the ETC-420-GX-2 in the storeroom already working on the tintelage, but the room was empty. Eight boxes sat in the middle of the floor. Henry knew a shipment that big would take all afternoon. He was in the middle of the third box when the human unit finally showed up to help.

Help? Henry thought with disgust, standing up. It should be *doing* the whole thing. "I've already finished reddishnesses 3138A1 and 3138B2."

"Hey, good job," the human said with a smile as he walked past the boxes to the supply shelves.

Henry couldn't believe his sight sensors. The ETC-420-GX-2 was wearing a Shine Bar signature logo fannypack. A human unit in a fannypack! That was insane. Humans didn't even have fans!

Things around there were definitely out of control.

Time to fix that. "I'm halfway through yellowishness 4149A1," he said.

The ETC-420-GX-2 picked up a white glass jar, examined the label and put it back. "Great."

"So the rest shouldn't take you too long," Henry added when it became clear the human hadn't gotten the hint. No surprise.

The unit glanced up as it reached for another jar. "Oh, I'm not here to unpack the boxes. I'm looking for Linoleum Infusion in Happy Taffy for Mrs. Leadfoot's waxing. It's her third treatment in three days. She says this is her home away from home. And here it is. Right next to Linoleum Infusion in Laughing Lollypop just like Steve said it would be. I'll see you later, right?"

Rage simmered through Henry, barely pausing in his emotionality stabilizer before racing to his circuits. The *human* was helping Steve. The *human* was learning treatments. The *human* was talking to customers.

The *human* was doing *Henry's* job!

And *Henry* was doing the *human's* job.

Oh, no. No. No. No.

Henry kicked the half-empty box, as his stabilizer downgraded the rage to fury. From there it was a short hop to anger, where it settled nicely and safely.

Calm now, he left the storeroom to register his complaint with his mom. He saw the ETC-420-GX-2 mixing an emulsion for Mrs. Leadfoot. Then Henry watched amazed as the human smeared the sticky substance on the client's frame. The ETC-420-GX-2 was performing treatments! Henry had never been allowed to perform treatments. Only licensed beautybots could do that.

When the human unit finished, Mrs. Leadfoot tossed him some coins.

Tips? The kitchen gadget was getting tips now?

Henry had never gotten a single half-credit coin from a customer.

It was unacceptable. Did his mom really think he was incapable of smearing stupid wax serum on a stupid client? A human could do it, but her own son wasn't up to the challenge? Did that mean she thought her own son was dumber than a human? That he was *less* than human?

Would she rather have an appliance for a son than her own child?

His emotionality stabilizer whirred as it struggled to manage the swirl of emotions. Renewed anger. Sadness. Embarrassment.

"I'm so impressed, Jane," Mrs. Leadfoot said. "Wherever did you get it?"

"My husband's office," his mother said, stopping to chat, although she clearly didn't have the time. Her management protocols stressed one-on-one interaction with customers as the best way to instill brand loyalty. "To be honest, I'm impressed too. As I'm sure you're aware, we had a minor unfortunate incident here a week ago involving a human and I was very reluctant to install one in my home. But it's a marvel."

"Modern technology is amazing," Mrs. Leadfoot said.

"Isn't it?" Jane agreed. "Now if you'll excuse me, my four o'clock dent amelioration just arrived and I need the ETC-420-GX-2 to set up the device."

Hold on—the *human* was setting up the dent ameliorator?

No, Henry thought, not while there was a charge left in his frame.

He marched over to the dent ameliorator, a small machine with a rotating disk. The disk slipped into a plastic casing that served as a handle so that beautybots could easily glide the disk along a bot's frame. The fragile device broke easily if not used correctly. The casing often shattered when too much pressure was applied or the lock snapped if you tried to force the disk in place.

Henry had been setting it up for two years and had broken it only once—and his mom knew that wasn't his fault. The beautybot hadn't cleaned off the silk cream, per usage instructions, and the greasy machine slipped from his grasp. There was no way a human could have the skill, delicacy and dexterity to assemble it properly.

Henry felt the casing to make sure it had been wiped down after its last use. Then he picked up the disk to insert it.

"That's cool, bro, I got it," the human said, grabbing the casing.

Just seeing the way its fingers clutched the delicate alloy convinced Henry that the human wasn't capable of the task. He reached for the casing. "I'm doing it."

The human didn't let go. "But your mom told me to."

"And now I'm telling you different," Henry said.

Still the human held on. "But it's no big deal. I can do it in a jiffy. And you've got all those boxes to unpack."

At the mention of boxes, Henry felt his energy surge

and he tugged forcefully on the casing. The human yanked it back just as roughly.

Crack!

The brand-new ameliorator splintered into a dozen pieces. Henry and the ETC-420-GX-2 looked at the mess on the floor, then at each other, then at Jane, who was barreling down on the both of them.

"Henry Arthur Jacobson, into the storeroom now," she said, her voice modulator set to QUIET MENANCE.

"But it's not my—"

"I said, into the storeroom now."

"But what about the ETC—"

"Henry," she added warningly.

His head lowered, he dragged his feet into the storeroom. His mom didn't immediately follow. She lingered a moment to instruct the human to clean up the mess and to make a joke about disobedient children to her clients. When she did come into the room, there was none of the jovial manager in her demeanor.

"I asked you to unpack the boxes, didn't I?" she said, her brusque tone letting him know that he was in for an interrogation.

"Yes," he muttered, although technically that wasn't true. It hadn't been a question but an order.

"And did you finish unpacking the boxes?"

She could see all the unpacked boxes herself, but he knew she still expected an answer. "No."

"No, there are six unpacked boxes. Why are there six unpacked boxes?"

"Because I didn't do them."

"And why didn't you do them?"

"Because I wanted to help out in the spa," he said.

His mom nodded. "Did I say I needed help in the spa?"

"No," he mumbled.

"What was that? I didn't hear you," Jane said.

"No, you didn't say you needed help in the spa. But

the dent ameliorator is very fragile and you know a human can't be trusted to—"

"I'm done talking about it, Henry," his mom said. "I've moved on to your punishment."

"Punishment? But I was only—"

"No comic books, television or video games for five days. Only homework and microchip-enriching magazines. Is that understood?"

Henry nodded silently, not that it mattered. The punishment would stand even if he didn't understand.

"Good. Now finish unpacking those boxes."

Henry dragged himself over to the box. "What about the ETC-420-GX-2?"

His mom paused with her hand on the door. "What about it?"

"What's its punishment?"

Suddenly, Jane's face softened and warmth infused her voice. "Oh, honey, it doesn't get a punishment. A human doesn't learn or grow or develop. It's an appliance. It'd be like punishing a cup of T. You understand the difference, don't you? You understand that the human's not alive?"

Henry nodded. He knew the difference between himself and a cup of T. He also knew the difference between himself and the salon's old Drudgery unit. But he wasn't so clear about the difference between himself and the ETC-420-GX-2. It wasn't alive like him, but it seemed alive enough to be grounded.

Reassured, his mother smiled. "Good. Finish up and we'll go home."

As Henry unpacked the boxes, he tried to evaluate his feelings. On the face of it, his resentment of the ETC-420-GX-2 was illogical. But when he ran it through the reasonator, it came back as LOGICAL. He tried his mother's trick and substituted a cup of T. In that case the reasonator returned the expected answer: ILLOGICAL.

The only conclusion Henry could reach was his reasonator was busted.

During the next two days, three hours, forty-nine minutes and eight seconds, every diagnostic he ran came back clean. His reasonator checked out. His reality affirmulator checked out. Even the diagnostic apparatus itself checked out. Baffled, he sat on his bed and stared at the wall. If his operating system was running fine, then his evaluation of the human was accurate. But he knew that couldn't be.

So he sat and stared.

His mother had replaced his comics with a stack of *Better Bot* magazines. He tried scanning an issue, but it had an eight-page article on organizing your fannypack. He couldn't bear it. The story was so boring. No, it was worse than boring. It was…. It was….

He remembered the ETC-420-GX-2's game of making up words and tried to think of a new one to describe a type of boredom so boring it was beyond bored.

It took him eight minutes and forty-six seconds. Then finally he came up with *benumbed.*

From the Near Central *be* meaning "having the state, quality, identity, etc" and Near Central *numb* meaning "deprived of the power of sensation."

That was it exactly. Reading *Better Bot* magazine was benumbing. It was the most crashed-out he'd ever felt with his sight sensors still open.

Delighted with his new word, Henry used it in a bunch of sentences. Then he tried to come up with another. It was difficult because he wasn't designed to make things up. Like all robots, his behavior, decisions and thoughts were programmed to follow precise protocols. Nobot strayed from his protocols.

By contrast, the human didn't seem to have any protocols at all. It simply did whatever it wanted whenever it wanted to.

The concept was so foreign, Henry couldn't wrap his chip around it.

A knock sounded on his door.

"Come in," he said, expecting his mom to pop in and announce dinner.

But it was the ETC-420-GX-2 holding a green plastic bag. "Hey."

"Hay," Henry said back.

"So...um...how's it going?" it asked.

Henry shrugged.

The human nodded. "Listen, I want to apologize for the way the ameliorator incident went down. The ameliorator's your thing; you've assembled it dozens of times. I should have stepped back and given you your space. I'm sorry you got punished for it. It was really my fault. I tried explaining that to your mom, but she wouldn't listen."

For the first time in two days, nine hours, fifty-one minutes and twenty seconds Henry smiled as he pictured his mother fielding an apology from a cup of T.

The ETC smiled back. "Hey, I know they cleaned you out of the good stuff, so I smuggled in a little contraband." He tossed the bag to Henry and half a dozen comic books slipped out. "I got the new MegaBot, number 274: *MegaBot Versus the Medusa Monster.* The rest are ones that looked interesting to me. But if you have requests I can go back tomorrow."

Once again, Henry was speechless. After a moment, he managed a baffled "How?"

"It was easy. I had my tips and the comic book store is only three doors down from the spa."

Henry stared at the collection of comic books. Along with the MegaBot there were two Batbots, one Botinator, one Fearless Freddy and an Odd Botkins.

"I got that one"—he pointed to the Odd Botkins—"because it had humans on the cover."

The cover in fact had an army of humans on it. Odd Botkins was a mad scientist who was always trying to take over the world using human technology. Every attempt he made was foiled by his son, a sixth-upgrader named Edd Botkins who wanted his dad to stop seeking world domination and play helioball with him. Each issue ended with little Eddy throwing a flamer in the air and saying, "Can we play *now*?"

It was one of Henry's favorite.

"They're humbies," he explained. "Human zombies. Odd invented them in number 37. This one's a classic. They're supposed to attack New Vanadium City, but Eddy teaches them how to play helioball and they go on to win the World Cup. How did you find it? I've been looking for it for months."

The human shrugged as its protein alloy frame turned bright pink. "No special trick. It was there on the shelf."

Henry arranged all six comic books in a neat pile that he clutched in both hands. He was more confused than ever. This human—this modern home appliance sold by the thousands in HueMarts everywhere—had found a store, selected a bunch of comic books and counted out enough change to buy them. That it had the cognitive and motor function to pull it off was amazing.

And yet that wasn't the staggering part. The staggering part was the reason it did it. Henry tried it one more time: apology, comic books, cup of T.

No, the ETC-420-GX-2 and a cup of T weren't the same. The human was alive enough for remorse. It was alive enough for restitution.

It was alive enough.

CHAPTER TEN
MILITARY RAMIFICATIONS

When Jacob came home from work a week later and announced a family meeting, Henry and the ETC-420-GX-2—or simply E, as Henry insisted on calling the unit—were playing *Mission Commander Scout Squad 4: Mission to Save the World from King John.*

"Incoming," Henry yelled in warning, as a King John Night Brigadier leapt out from behind the Tarsium Nebula to attack E's scout ship.

E whipped his console rod to the left and shook it once. Green light streaked across the screen.

A hit!

Ship down!

"Bravo, scout," Mission Commander Nickelby said, his face flickering against the blackness of deep inner space.

"Wow. You got 9,999 points for that," Henry said.

"The ship was carrying ultraviolet radiation ionises," E reminded him. "That's worth triple."

Henry knew that. He also knew the hit put E in the lead.

But not for long. He had his own ionises-carrying brigadier in his sight finder. All he had to do was line up the shot and take it. He twirled his rod; his ship spun through the air.

The screen of the Melpitude CP-2000 blazed with light, and Henry tightened his hold on the ControlPole, a six-inch-long rod that fit comfortably in his grasp. The Melp was the best unit on the market—a state-of-the-art machine that transmitted algorithmic codes directly to a twenty-inch glassed screen, which flashed brightly with a rainbow of colors; the CP-2000 could be loaded with thousands of different video games.

"I said family meeting," Jacob announced.

Henry didn't spare him a glance. "Almost done."

"Where's your mom?"

"Upstairs. Knitting."

As Jacob dashed up the steps, Henry aimed his proton gun at a wormhole and shot. A brigadier zipped out and clipped his right wing. His spaceship slipped into a spiral and crashed into a meteor.

"Aww. I'm dead."

"Still in," E said, his eyes bobbing right and left as more and more shards of light attacked the squad. "Just need to…." A loud explosion followed a bright, shimmering glow. "I'm out. Those Star Slices get me every time."

"Yeah, but you got the high score," Henry said excitedly.

His parents came down the stairs. "No more games. We're having a family meeting," Jacob said.

Henry looked at E and made a face. Family meetings were boring. He didn't know what this one was about, but previous topics included how to improve Henry's grades and where to find Henry a tutor.

Jacob stood while Jane sat on the sofa. He seemed very excited as if he had a big announcement to make. "As you know, installing the ETC-420-GX-2 was a special request from the Motherboard. We were reluctant at first to bring a human appliance into our home, but to everyone's satisfaction it has worked out extremely well. So well, in fact, that I talked to the Yet Another Seat today and proposed a plan to—"

Henry's circuits almost shorted from the shock. "You talked to Mission Commander Nickelby?"

His father smiled. "We had a meeting, yes."

"Flickering Flames! That is so amped!" he exclaimed, his excitement meter racing to THOROUGHLY, UNBEARABLY, OVERWHELMINGLY EXCITED. His sight sensors glowed as he turned to E. "Did you hear that? He *met* the commander. What was he like? What did he say? Was he wearing his Metal of Distinction? Was it so shiny it was blinding?"

"Henry," Jane said, voice modulator set to EXPLAINING ONE PLUS ONE TO A GOOSENECK LAMP, "how many times have I told you the human can't maintain conversation?"

"But he can—"

"And how many times have I told you not to use the generic male pronoun?" she asked. "He's an it. An *it*. Please say *it*."

"But, Mom, he—"

Jane grunted.

Jacob raised a calming hand. "Let's not get bogged down in a familiar discussion. For the last time, Henry, please stop talking to the human as if it were capable of ratiocination. It is an inanimate object. Now, as I was saying, I had a meeting today with Mr. Nickelby."

As eager as he was to hear about his dad's meeting with Mission Commander Nickelby, Henry couldn't suppress his own exasperation. All week his parents had been criticizing his interaction with E. It made no sense. First they wanted him to get over his fear of the human, then they wanted him to get some of it back. Clearly, they didn't know what they wanted.

"You didn't mention a meeting at breakfast," his mom said.

"It was unscheduled. I ran into Mr. Nickelby on the elevator and initiated conversation," he explained. "I'd never seen him around the Circuit Tree before so I knew it was a special opportunity."

"And he knew who you were?" Jane asked.

"No, not at first. In fact, it seemed as if he'd never heard of the ETC-420-GX-2, myself, Mr. Erickson or the assignment. I had to explain in great detail and very quickly because a G-bot on his security detail was leading me away by my elbow. But once I described all the amazing things the ETC could do, his memory bank accessed the information and he wanted to know everything. We went back to his office and talked about the human's accomplishments for twenty-eight minutes. He was quite impressed with what I've managed to do with it so far, so I volunteered to spearhead a series of experiments to better identify and quantify its various functions. He thinks this is a great idea and is looking forward to my report with all the enthusiasm his emotionality stabilizer will allow. Do you know what this means?"

"I get to meet him?" Henry asked.

"A promotion," his mom said.

"Branch manager," Jacob confirmed.

"And from there you can go anywhere. The sky's the limit," she excitedly.

"Maybe Under-Seat of Law, or even Cushion."

Henry couldn't believe that on the day his father met the most famous robot on the planet all his parents could talk about was his *job*. It was as if, to them, Nickelby was just another government official. Henry tried to get the important details from his father, but all he would talk about was the report he had to prepare.

"When's it due?" his mother asked.

While Jacob talked about due dates, Henry looked at E and tilted his head as if to say, Let's go; there's no need to listen to this conversation.

E agreed with a nod. The two got up and walked toward the stairs.

"Where are you going?" Jacob asked, breaking off midsentence.

"To play MARFELs," Henry said, mentioning the new game E had invented using his meal pellets. The rules were simple: Arrange thirteen round pills in the center of a chalk circle, then try to hit as many as you can out of the circle using another MARFEL. The player with the most MARFELs at the end won. It sounded easy but was surprisingly hard.

E had also invented MARFEL Walk, which required players to walk on the MARFELs from one side of the room to the other without falling. Each time a player tapped the opposite wall, he scored a point.

It continued to surprise Henry how E could just make stuff up at random. With robots, it was only those loaded with invention protocols who had the ability to create new things. Dr. Felix J. Tinsmith, the bot who invented humans, for example, had algorithms specifically encoded for the construction of new devices. But he never strayed from his identified goal. He worked the mission.

E came up with his own mission.

Jacob shook his head as Henry headed for the stairs. "We're in the middle of a family meeting."

"Only in the middle?" Henry muttered. "You mean we're just halfway through?"

His father gave him a stern look. "This is a very serious matter, and I trust you will treat it with the gravity it deserves. I'm about to offer you a job."

Henry rolled his eyes. Great. Another chore.

"I want you to help me develop a set of tests," Jacob announced.

Henry's surprise meter shot straight to SUPER SURPRISED. "Me?"

"Yes, you. Watching you play *Mission Commander Scout Squad* with the ETC-420-GX-2 made me grasp the full potential of human technology," his father explained. "Competing against the human improved your skills, making you a stronger competitor. In addition, it advanced your etiquette protocols. Previously, you've shown poor sportsmanship behavior when you lose, a system glitch your mother and I tried with little success to override. But now you grasp the importance of a legitimate challenge and accept losing as part of the game. These are important tactical advancements and protocol improvements, which the Federal Agency of Observation and Reportation could benefit from. The military ramifications of the new technology are huge."

"You mean human technology could be employed as a weapon of war?" Jane asked.

Henry heard the words *weapon of war* but didn't process them. All his reasonator could handle at the moment was the notion that he might work on a project with Mission Commander Nickelby. They would be almost like *partners*.

While Jacob explained that a viable human weapon was still decades away, Henry visualized going into school the next day and informing everyone that he was on special assignment for Mission Commander Nickelby. Evan would blow a circuit.

"What do you say, Henry?" his father asked. "Ready to sign on as my assistant?"

Henry's head bounced up and down. "Yes, sir. We"— he looked at E as he spoke—"are eager to be of service."

If E didn't show the same enthusiasm to be of service or if his external skin organ had turned unusually white at the words *weapon of war*, Henry didn't process that either. He was working on a project with Mission Commander Nickelby. He was a Commander Scout for real now.

Best. Day. Ever.

REPORT #JJ001

Prepared by Jacob Jacobson
Department Head
Upgrade Processing
Central Processing Unit

Summary The subject responds to all experiments with unprecedented proficiency. Upon examination, it was able to maintain multiple functions at once, follow complex commands, adapt to its surroundings and process logically. The examiner concludes that the subject is worth further study to discover practical applications for its use.

Subject HueManTech unit # ETC-420-GX-2
Examiner Jacob Jacobson
Purpose To assess the strengths and weaknesses of the subject
Model of study Provide experiments for the subject and gauge how well it performs

Experiment #1 The subject is given a piece of gummy plastic to chew, then asked to walk to the other side of the room.

Skill Multiple-function maintenance
Performance The subject successfully negotiated the walk to the other side of the room while chewing the gum. Furthermore, it did not swallow or choke on the piece of gum.
Conclusion The subject is capable of performing multiple functions at once.

Experiment #2 The subject is told to remember the word *crystallization.* Then it is given a sheet of paper and a pencil. The examiner reads aloud a sentence from that day's news download while the subject writes it down on paper. The subject is then asked to repeat the word.
Skill Advanced multiple-function maintenance; attention span; fine motor skills
Performance The subject successfully remembered the word *crystallization* after transcribing the sentence in longhand.
Conclusion The subject is capable of performing multiple advanced functions at once. It can maintain its concentration for a brief period of time. The subject also has a clear, steady hand as well as neat, easy-to-read penmanship.

Experiment #3 The subject is led to a location one-quarter mile from the examiner's house. The subject is told to wait ten minutes, then return home.
Skills Temporal understanding; distance perception; memory; spatial relations
Performance After waiting 60 seconds, the subject walked in the opposite direction of the examiner's house. The subject turned left off Hard Drive, continued straight for three-quarters of a mile, then turned right onto Disk Drive. At 2:37, the subject entered Berrylium's Emporium and Hardware and bought a container of gummy plastic. Then it walked home.
Conclusion The subject's sense of direction is strong. It can remember where it has been and can draw a map in

its cortextinator to chart the path. Its sense of time is less developed. Its internal clock operates ten times as fast as regular time. The examiner suggests that the subject be given a watch until this malfunction can be corrected.

Experiment #4 The subject is brought into the kitchen and instructed to sit at the table. The examiner lights a towel on fire, drops it on the table and leaves.
Skills Problem-solving; cognitive function; motor skills
Performance The subject successfully extinguished the fire by dowsing it with a bottle of Go-Go Pep Solution.
Conclusion The subject's cognitive function is high. It demonstrates a basic understanding of fire, self-preservation and respect for property. The subject's motor skills, both gross and fine, are well-developed. The subject can manipulate small objects and perform various hand-eye-coordination tasks. However, it shows an inexplicable preference for its right hand and seems incapable of performing many tasks with its left hand.

Experiment #5 The subject is given the first chapter of *The Theory of Robotivity* to scan and is asked a series of questions regarding the content.
Skills Scanning comprehension; attention span; information retention; ability to reason
Performance The subject successfully completed the chapter in a reasonable thirty-four minutes. It answered nine out of ten of the questions correctly. The subject did not agree with Dr. Einsteinium's theory that the speed of a robot in a vacuum depends on the speed of the observer. Instead, it kept insisting that the speed of the robot is the same regardless.
Conclusion The subject is capable of concentrating for long periods of time and can comprehend what it scans. Its ability to grasp complex scientific concepts is somewhat impaired.

CHAPTER ELEVEN
THE ONLY WAY TO STOP A TRUCK

When Henry arrived at the Shine Bar for his Wednesday shift, his mother looked completely frazzled. Her sight sensors flickered erratically as she flipped haphazardly through her clipboard.

"Of course I have it right here," she said, pointing vaguely at the schedule. "Mrs. Elmira Curiumette. Tint. Three-thirty."

"I knew I had an appointment," she said, casting an angry glare at the receptionbot, who glared back.

Jane glanced briefly at her obstinate employee—all clients had an appointment, even those who didn't—then back to Mrs. Curiumette. "Of course you did. Now, if you wouldn't mind waiting for only a moment, I'll have someone take you immediately."

Mrs. Curiumette pursed her lips but agreed to sit down.

"Hay," Henry said, sliding his backpack off his shoulder. "Busy day. I hope E had time for his breaks."

Jane swung around and stared at her son, as if shocked to see him. "Henry, what are you doing here?"

"It's Wednesday. I'm always here on Wednesday," he said. His mother was beyond frazzled if she didn't know what day of the week it was.

"Right, yes. *Wednesday.*" She smiled weakly. "We're not that busy today, so I'm not going to need you. Thanks for coming in and I'll see you at home."

Henry looked at his mother as if she had a bolt loose. Not busy? The place was *packed.*

Suddenly, a green-tinted hand waved in his face. It belonged to the Zippy 12.6 model standing next to his mom. "Talley-ho Terbiumor, ace newsbot for the *Sodium Gazette,*" she announced.

"She's doing a robot-interest story on the spa," Jane explained.

"I'm covering the human," the newsbot said and wiggled her fingers when Henry failed to shake her hand. "You're Henry, right?"

Henry nodded and took her hand.

His mother stepped between them. "And to try out our treatments, I hope. Our realignment special is the best in town."

Talley-ho shook her head. "Bribes are against the paper's policy."

"I didn't mean—"

Whatever his mom didn't mean was cut off by the newsbot. "Word spreads pretty quickly in a town this small, you know what I'm saying? We in the daily download biz look for something we call a story with wheels. You know what a story with wheels is?"

Henry couldn't tell if she was asking him or his mom,

but since she didn't expect an answer he didn't worry about it. "A story with wheels is one that travels. Goes far, see? And this story about a super human has half a dozen wheels. You know what that means?"

This time she stopped and looked at Henry. "Uh, no."

"It's a truckmobile. A truck goes fast. It barrels into things. You know the only way to stop a truck? Run it into a brick wall. Now tell me, son, what do you think is the most impressive thing about the ETC-420-GX-2?"

Henry didn't even have to think about it. "He can clear the fortieth level—"

"ShineGuard Wax," Jane said, her tone loud and shrill.

Talley-ho and Henry looked at her in surprise.

"ShineGuard Wax," she said again. "There's a big box of it in the storeroom, and it needs to be unpacked right now. It's an emergency."

Although Henry couldn't conceive of any situation that would qualify as a ShineGuard emergency, he said OK and headed to the back room. He would have liked to talk to Talley-ho about how cool E was, but he didn't want to be around his mom while she was acting so strangely. Obviously, something about the newsbot frayed her wires. He'd never seen her in any mode other than TOTALLY IN CHARGE and found the experience disconcerting.

E was helping with a buff 'n' shine, and he waved to Henry, who pointed to the door to the storeroom and opened his palm. Five minutes. E nodded.

The massively urgent box of ShineGuard wax was tucked away in the far corner, with a shipping label that clearly stated it had been there for over a week. Henry shrugged and dug into the box.

A few minutes later, E came in. "Hey, what's up?"

Henry held up a jar. "ShineGuard fun."

E dropped to the floor next to him and reached for a jar. "It feels good to sit down. Things have been crazy. But I am raking in the tips. Clients like throwing change at me to see if I can catch it. I drop a few to keep up the suspense."

Henry laughed. He'd seen his friend pretending to bobble the coins, and it was hilarious. "Has the newsbot been here all day?"

"Only since one," he said. "Threw your mom into a tizzy. Apparently, she's been trying to get the *Sodium Gazette* to cover the spa for three years, and then a newsbot drops by unannounced."

"She's here to cover you," Henry said. "Have you talked to her yet?"

E shook his head. "She's in INFO-GATHERING mode. She observes what I do, then makes a note in her pad. Then she interviews everyone about what I've just done. The staff are under strict orders to talk up the treatments. The employee who convinces her to try one gets next week off. What about you?"

"I met her on the way in," Henry said. "I was about to tell her how you've cleared the fortieth level of *Mission Commander* and I can't get past thirty-eight, but Mom sent me back here."

E's smile gleamed in the florescent light of the storeroom. "It's talent. Either you have it or you don't."

"Either *you* have it or you don't," Henry said. "*I* can always upload it at my next upgrade."

"Yeah, I'd like to see that."

"You're on. As soon as——"

The door swung open and Talley-ho entered. "Henry, I know you've got important unpacking to do, but I figured you're smart enough to handle talking and unpacking at the same time. Whaddaya say?"

"OK."

Talley-ho dragged a box from against the wall and sat down. "When we talked earlier, you said…" Here she paused to hit PLAY on her recording app and Henry heard his own voice enthusing, "He can clear the fortieth level." Then she continued. "Am I correct in assuming the *he* you are refering to is in fact the ETC-420-GX-2?"

"Yes."

"So you think of the ETC-420-GX-2 as a *he*?"

Again, Henry said yes.

"Why is that?" she asked.

Henry looked briefly at E, then said, "He's my friend."

Talley-ho nodded, recording the data with her note-taking app. "Elaborate."

"Elaborate what?" Henry said, confused.

"Talk about your friendship. What do you do together?"

Henry shrugged. "I don't know. Everything."

"Like what?"

"Video games. Comic books. MARFELs. Sometimes we talk."

"What about?"

"I don't know. I explain things."

"Such as?"

"How to play helioball."

Talley-ho smiled. "And just to be absolutely clear, let me ask this: Do you understand that the ETC-420-GX-2 is different from you? Do you understand that it's a human and you're a robot? That basic fact isn't beyond your processing capabilities?"

"I know he's different from me," Henry said. This inteview was just like the conversations he'd had with his parents in recent days. They kept emphasizing the idea of different. He got that. He knew that he and E had different circuitry. But in all the ways that mattered they were the same. "But he's not really."

"So you're saying—"

"Henry!" Jane stood horrified in the doorway. "I thought I told you to set up the ameliorator. Mrs. McMercury is waiting!"

Henry jumped to his feet and scurried out the room. He'd been told no such thing—since the incident, he hadn't even been allowed to *look* at the ameliorator—but his mother was clearly not in the mood to be contradicted.

84

While Henry handled the fragile machine with extra delicacy, he saw E mixing an emulsion for Steve. Talley-ho stood a few feet away, watching.

Suddenly, a scream filled the spa. Before the last note of the cry had sounded, Jane was at the traumatized client's side, assuring Mrs. Silverberg that the bright red spot in the middle of her forehead would be removed immediately. "All our products are one hundred percent natural and will cause no lasting damage," she said, her voice modulator set to PLEASE KEEP MOVING—NOTHING TO SEE HERE.

But it wasn't that simple. Instead of spilling Reddishness 6658Z1, Pierre had spilled Redlike 474GA, a lacquer for his furniture-decorating class. The two bottles looked exactly alike except for the shape of the labels. "I'm so sorry. I got distracted. It's been a long afternoon, and I didn't get my afternoon break."

The staff lounge had been permanently turned into a waiting room annex, a change that obviously hadn't gone over very well with the staff.

Jane continued to assure the woman, whose daughter's networking ceremony was in four hours, that an easy solution would be found and in the meantime would she please enjoy a free waxing and realignment?

Talley-ho and her notebook marched over to beautystation 4. Carefully, she copied down all the information on the 474GA label.

Henry's mother pressed her offer for complimentary services, throwing in free monthly buff 'n' shines for a year.

The distraught mother of the bridebot began to mumble, "I'm marked for life. I'm marked for life."

"Stop whining. It's a big dot in the middle of your head. So what. Stick a fannypack over it and move on," snapped Elmira Curiumette, who took off her own pack and impatiently strapped it to the victim's head.

As a stain hider, the fannypack worked nicely, but it also covered Mrs. Silverberg's sight sensors and had the added benefit of looking absurd, a fact that Pierre immediately pointed out. Several robots insisted it didn't look all that awful and if you could cut holes in the fannypack, then she could see. Pierre protested, Elmira snickered, and the debate grew louder and louder.

Henry looked over to E to see if he also thought the red-red scandal was hilarious, but E was engrossed in the discussion.

"Hey," E said to no one in particular, "turn it into a tattoo."

The room fell silent. Talley-ho flipped to a fresh page. Jane said, "A what?"

"A tattoo. From the Distant Northern *tatau* meaning 'mark,' " he explained. "Turn the dot into a pretty design. It'll be like tinting but with a picture."

"I can do florettes," Pierre offered.

Jane's sight sensors began to flicker again. "I don't think—"

"Florettes?" Mrs. Silverberg said. "Like a gypsum rosette or a carnelian violet?"

Pierre reached for a pen. "I can do whatever you want. What kind of crystals is your daughter carrying? We can match her bouquet."

"Rosettes," she said, her voicing rising with excitement.

"Classic," Pierre exclaimed as he drew one.

Twenty minutes later, Mrs. Silverberg was eagerly getting her first tattoo while everyone in the spa watched. Jane tried several times to get her staff to return to their stations, but they didn't budge. They were too busy watching Pierre paint lovely little rosettes onto the client's head. When he was done, he stood back to admire his handiwork. Everyone had to admit it looked pretty good. Even Elmira Curiumette was heard to mutter, "Not completely disfiguring."

As soon as Mrs. Silverberg stood up, another client, one scheduled for a simple buff 'n' shine, sat down at Pierre's station and said, "Me next. Me next." She wanted three little quartz icicles under her shoulder joint in back.

Pierre immediately began to sketch examples.

"That was amazing," Henry said to E. "How did you know it would work?"

E shrugged. "Lucky guess."

The concept of guessing was completely alien to Henry. Robots could deduce and conject, but they didn't have an algorithm for reaching entirely unsupported conclusions. But he knew what his friend meant.

"I want one," he said. "Do you think I should?"

"Totally," E said.

Excited, Henry tracked down his mom. She was in her office drawing up a price list: Small tattooes cost thirty credits, large fifty.

"Hay," he said, poking only his head into the room, "can I get one?"

Jane didn't look up. "I can't do this right now. We'll talk about it at home later."

Henry didn't know what there was to talk about. *Can I get a tattoo* was a simple yes-or-no question—and since his mom hadn't said no yet, he continued to make his case. "Pretty, pretty please. I'll come in every day next week for free, and I'll come in on Saturday, and I'll come in on *Sunday* and clean the entire spa from top to bottom. I'll even do the windows. And I'll reorganize the storeroom. The tints should be in the front and the—"

His mom waved her hand impatiently. "OK, OK, you can get a tattoo."

Henry whooped gleefully. "Really? I can?"

"Yes, yes. Now please close the door on the way out. I *have* to get this done."

"Right, sure. I'll let you finish that." He pulled the door closed, then thought better of it and opened it again. "Only, do I have to come in on Sunday? E and I are going to a Sodium Falls Oil Slicks helioball game."

"Henry…" she said warningly without looking up.

He knew that tone and quickly shut the door before she changed her mind—or, worse, decided they should consult his dad first. Jacob wouldn't go for a tattoo. His programming was too traditional. He'd never even gotten a tint treatment, which was a standard beauty protocol.

87

With no time to spare, Henry ran to put his name on Pierre's list, now two pages long. While he waited, he bounced tattoo ideas off E. Obviously, he'd get a Commander Scout Squad tag but the question was which one. E pushed for the Mission to Save the World from King John insignia. Henry, however, had never completed that mission and didn't feel like he earned the emblem. He'd won the Mission to Save the World from Warlord Wally 4,639 times but that mission was so easy he'd be embarrassed to show up with the insignia at school.

"What about a Metal of Distinction?" Pierre suggested, sketching quickly. "We could do it in black, so it'll really pop off your silver frame."

Henry nodded eagerly. *Pop* was exactly what he wanted.

Pierre pulled a bottle of black from the shelf and began applying the laminate. It took him only ten minutes to paint the one-inch design on Henry's upper arm. When the tattoo was done, Henry ran over to show E. His friend immediately agreed it was great, and they stood in front of the mirror admiring it for more than a minute.

"It really does pop," E said.

"I know," Henry said.

They smiled at each other in perfect agreement.

Suddenly a bright light flashed in Henry's sight sensor, blinding him for a split second. When his vision cleared, he saw Talley-Ho Terbiumor triumphantly waving a camera. "Got it," she said, examining the shot with satisfaction. "Thanks, boys. Call me if you want extra copies of the article."

Before Henry could respond, she zipped up her fannypack and left.

Sodium Gazette Exclusive!
Shine Bar Gets New Appliance—
Is This the End of the World As We Know It?

By Talley-Ho Terbiumor

The question on everyone's processor at the Shine Bar Spa & Boutique on Disk Drive isn't: Who does your tints? It's: Where can I get one of those? The "those" in question is a human that functions better than any human unit you've ever seen in a HueManTech catalog. When news of this "super" human reached my sound sensors, I knew I had to pay a visit to the beauty establishment to check out the phenomenon myself. Here's what I discovered when I dropped by last week.

The Shine Bar is a seemingly unremarkable storefront in the heart of Sodium Falls's bustling business district, not at all the sort of place you'd expect to find a possible worldwide cabal intent on destroying robotkind.

Like many of its kind, the Shine Bar relies on the obvious trappings of relaxation: dim lights, warm scents, a calm hum like your mother's processor following you everywhere you go. In its six treatment rooms you can get an oiling, a waxing, a dent amelioration or a realignment massage. In the front are ten beautystations for tinting, buffing and polishing.

The spa usually does a brisk business, although in recent weeks it had fallen off, thanks to an unfortunate berserko-human incident.

"It was terrifying," says Carmen, a sixth-upgrade teachbot who dropped by for a quick burnishing after work. "The thing was completely out of control. It was throwing chairs, mirrors, tint jars, anything it could get its hands on. I barely escaped with my life."

Other clients tell a similar tale of stark terror and share fears of returning. They had resolved to stay away and yet here they were at the spa just as I was. What brought them back?

"The ETC-420-GX-2," Carmen says emphatically.

Another client, Esther, agrees. "Everyone said the ETC-420-GX-2 had to be seen to be believed."

Jane Jacobson, manager of the spa and owner of the ETC-420-GX-2, is vague about its origins. "My husband got it from work," she says. "It was very useful around the house, so I thought it would be useful around the spa."

"Useful" is putting it mildly.

Unlike other units, the ETC-420-GX-2 can follow complex instructions. You can tell it to sweep the floor without first telling it to go to the storeroom in the back of the store to get the broom. It also has an unusually large memory. Two hours after I told it my name, it recalled it. Sources report that it is able to retain information for up to 24 hours.

"It brought me a cup of T sludge in crude because he remembered I liked it," Esther says. "It was a full day later. A *full day* later. My own son can't remember I like my T sludge crude."

By all accounts, this is definitely not your parents' human.

To find out more about its development, I contacted

HueManTech, unit's purported manufacturer. "We are very proud of our ETC line," says a spokesbot for the company, "and of our patented Cerebral Cortextinator technology." When pressed on the special skills of this particular ETC, the spokesbot insisted that all their units were special. "We call it quirkiness, and it's what makes every human unique."

Still, a trip to the local HueMart raised doubts that this ETC-420-GX-2 is even part of the HueManTech ETC line. It looks nothing like the other models, which have the typical slack-jawed design we've come to associate with later-model humans. It also has fewer speculative chronological years. Most ETCs are in the twenty-five to thirty-five range. This unit is twelve to fourteen.

Talking to other ETC unit owners confirms this suspicion. All of them express amazement when they hear what the ETC-420-GX-2 is capable of. Rosa, of Sodium Falls, owns the ETC-360-KX-1, which can sweep the floor and put the trash by the curb but can't bag the trash first or put away the broom. "And that's on a good day," Rosa says. "Sounds to me like someone put a super human into an ETC box to pass it off as a regular human."

Is the Jacobsons' unit a super human or a regular human having lots of very good days?

Elmira Curiumette, a regular at the Shine Bar, thinks a technological revolution is at hand. "Clearly this is a whole new level of human," she says, citing the unit's ability to invent words. But she doesn't think the innovations are good. "It's a weapon developed by the government. I wouldn't be surprised if one day it destroys us all."

Ciriumette's concerns might not be completely unfounded. On the day this newsbot was at the Shine Bar, the unit convinced an unsuspecting customer to undergo an untested and possibly dangerous process called tattooing, in which a lacquer paint is applied directly to the alloy coat.

The process has started a craze, with several dozen robots already undergoing treatment.

"We definitely need to investigate this," says Colin Strontiumstraub of the Maintenance Branch of the Circuit Tree. "At this moment, we don't know anything about this so-called tattooing. The number one question for me is, what kind of effect does the laminate have on various alloys? It could react differently to each one. What's fine for a pewter might be corrosive for a bulat steel. The problem is we don't know. Maybe it'll turn out to be harmless. Maybe I'll get a tattoo myself one day. But right now it's an unknown quantity and I don't like unknown quantities."

Hilda Silverberg, or Patient Zero, as the Maintenance Branch calls her, has suffered no ill effect so far but is worried about the future. "It might be years before we know the complete effects of this treatment," she says sadly. "All I can do is wait it out and hope for the best."

But others aren't as cautious and the spa continues to do tattoos at the rate of fifteen a day. "I think it's great," says Joshua, a seventeenth-upgrader at Sodium Falls High School who proudly showed off his new tattoo: a mopedmobile with a dagger stabbing its front wheel.

What could this dark imagery portend for the future of robotkind?

The representative from the Maintenance Branch shakes his head sadly. "I wish I knew. I wish to heck I knew."

Most worrisome of all is Jacobson's own son Henry's reaction to the human unit. The Sodium Falls Middle School student has developed what some would call a disturbingly close attachment to the ETC-420-GX-2. "He's my friend," says the recently upgraded Zaklad 5000. "We do lots of stuff together. We play video games and scan comic books. I'm teaching him helioball." When asked about the difference between himself and the human, the young boy gets confused. "I know he's different from me, but he's not really different."

Mark Zincton, a child pyschologist at the Rutherford Institute for Reality Disorders, the leading institution for the treatment of unreality conditions, believes the impressionable teen's confusion is a matter of grave concern. "The intergrational problems of the thirteenth upgrade are well documented and should never be underestimated. At best, this is a serious case of bent-reality syndrome, in which the reality affirmulator is unable to integrate the new realities of the operating system. At worst, it's a potentially disasterous case of a new and frightening technology rewriting a microchip or manipulating an operating system weakened by poor intergration."

For her part, Jane Jacobson is too busy enjoying her spa's success to worry about her son's fragile operating system. "I've never seen anything like this," she says, happily pointing to the crowded waiting room. "We're booked through next month, which is amazing. It's also amazing that so many bots want to try the ETC-420-GX-2. I think we tend to get jaded about technology, and then something like the ETC reminds us how far we've come."

So, I ask, she's not at all concerned that the human could be a weapon of mass destruction developed by our government or some shadowy organization with evil intentions as the Robothood of Peace had warned more than forty years ago?

Jacobson is taken aback, then laughs. "The ETC-420-GX-2? It's just a toy, an appliance. It can't hurt us."

She speaks with such unfettered confidence that, as my dollop of concern threatens to become a deluge of worry, I can't help envying her positive attitude and wondering, Where can I get one of those?

CHAPTER TWELVE
A PERFECTLY NORMAL ADOLESCENT PHASE

Henry waved his hand at a hovering E and told him to go away.

E refused and stood solidly next to him. "I should do it. They wouldn't notice me."

"Not *notice* you?" Henry asked, sight sensors blinking with impatience. "They're *talking* about you."

"Yeah, but they wouldn't think I shouldn't hear," E said reasonably. "I'm just an appliance."

Henry knew his friend was kidding, but he wasn't amused. All day bots had been saying that exact thing to him. It's just an appliance, Henry. It's just an appliance.

It had been the constant refrain at school—first Mrs. Yitteriumski, then the principal, then the nurse, then a sneaky newsbot from the *New Vanadium City Times* who

94

was promptly escorted from the premises by a guardbot. His classmates said it too, even the ones who'd dropped by the Shine Bar to see E in action. Sissy O'Thalium had been so impressed with E she followed him around for a half hour, asking him a dozen questions about everything he did. And yet she'd spent the day chanting, Lank Hank and the rank crank.

It was that stupid daily download story. Everything was fine until Talley-Ho Terbiumor published her lies: Danger! Secret Government Weapon Targets Small Town and Reprograms Teen Bot! Sets Sights on Rest of World! Nobot Is Safe!

It was so illogical, nobot could possibly believe it.

Except, *everybot* believed it.

His mom did. She was in the kitchen right now ordering Jacob to get rid of E. She tried to be secretive about it, but Henry and E easily figured out the topic of conversation, which was why they were arguing about who should listen. Henry was the obvious choice because he could raise the volume receptor on his sound sensors. E contended he could hear more by simply walking into the room as if nothing special were going on.

Like they'd talk *about* the human in *front* of the human! "Trust me," E said, "it happens all the time. They won't notice me. I'm part of the scenery."

Henry knew it was true, and it frazzled his microchip that other robots couldn't see what a fully formed being his friend was. There was no difference between him and E, except E had red fluid in his wires and Henry had copper piping.

He didn't expect the idiots at school to get it or even Mrs. Y, but his parents knew better. From the very beginning, they'd recognized E's enhanced capabilities. While Henry had been urging them to contact their service provider, they had him shaving lawns and fixing back doors.

And then as soon as one desperate, sensationalistic newsbot suggested E might be a weapon of mass destruction, his mom wanted him gone. It was completely illogical.

But Henry knew it wasn't. His mom's managerial protocols required her to blend into her community. A manager wasn't supposed to stand out; she was meant to fit in. She had the same white clapboard house as her neighbors, the same dusk-blooming nightlights lining the same stone walk. Her son was the only thing in her life that didn't comply with her codes. He was supposed to be a well-programmed machine who played helioball, performed glitchless integrations and had dozens of friends.

He did none of those things.

And now he considered an appliance to be his friend.

Jane couldn't handle the embarrassment. She was genuinely worried about him, of course, but her concern was mingled with mortification. Henry knew it, which made his own deep and abiding mortification worse.

"You *know* my parents wouldn't fall for the invisible-human trick. They know you're not just an appliance," Henry said, struggling to hear the low grumble of conversation on the other side of the door. Had his mother just said *sponge*? Huh? "You're making me miss the whole thing. Go away already."

"Fine. I'll go away," E muttered, slinking up the stairs with rounded shoulders and puckered lips. "It's not like it has anything to do with me. I'm just a gadget."

He was trying to make him feel bad, Henry realized, watching his friend disappear around the corner. He was using a guilt-trip app, just like his parents, even though he didn't have one.

How could *anyone* say he wasn't alive?

Annoyed at the predictable blindness of the whole entire world, Henry pressed his left sound sensor against the door to listen. The words were muffled. It was a risk, but he had to open it a crack. Very slowly, he turned the knob and tugged it toward him a fraction of an inch.

There, that was much better.

"... a little strange," his father was saying. "But lots of kids form attachments to inanimate objects. It's a perfectly normal adolescent phase."

"It's a perfectly normal adolescent phase to form an attachment to a ceramic brick or slab of granite, not a human," his mom said impatiently. "And it's more than an attachment. He thinks it's one of us. That's not normal. You saw what the doctor at the Rutherford said. His reality could be bent or twisted. What if the upgrade was too much for his system? What if it's interfering with his ability to process information? What if he crashes again? What if he has a permanent error?"

Henry tried to catch his dad's response, but the words were spoken too softly. Although he couldn't see what was going on, he knew his father was comforting her.

"… our fault?" his mom asked, her tone no calmer than before despite his dad's efforts. "We should have listened to him when he said the ETC was deranged. I swore we'd send it back at the first sign of trouble, but I was too busy enjoying the novelty of a functioning human unit to pay attention. That paranoia was an early manifestation of his malfunction, and we callously ignored it."

"Oh, no, honey, no. You're looking at this all wrong. Henry's suspicion was entirely natural. He'd just had a run-in with a berserko human, and his hazard meter was on high alert. I would have been worried if he hadn't thought something was wrong," he said evenly. "But on the whole, the human has been good for Henry. Ever since his virus, he's been a quiet and withdrawn child. The human has normalized his social programming. You were as pleased as I was with his progress. You even said the beautybots at the spa noticed the change."

Henry thought this was a very reasonable speech and cheered his father silently. But his mother went on like he hadn't said a word. "Or maybe it's worse than we ever speculated. Henry could've been right all along. His hazard meter might've been responding to subtle indications that ours weren't sensitive enough to pick up. We dismissed his concerns as random paranoia but what do we really know about that thing? I mean, what is it really? It's not a HueManTech ETC-420-GX-2. The newsbot was clear about that. And look at what it can do. It plays video games and makes up words. It speaks Extreme Southern.

Jacob, it replaced the bristles on the broom. Most robots can't do that."

"You're letting the article get to you."

"What if she's right?"

"The newsbot is trying to sell papers," his father pointed out to Henry's huge relief. Yes, he thought, let's talk about the newsbot's motives for a while. Her story wouldn't have been nearly as juicy if E wasn't some kind of secret government weapon bent on destroying them all. "Don't buy into the hysteria."

"Don't call me hysterical," his mom said, missing the point entirely.

"I said the *situation* was hysterical," Jacob said, his voice modulator turned to TRYING TO CONVINCE A LUMP OF COAL.

Henry's mom didn't appreciate his attitude. "You yourself said the ETC could be employed as a weapon of war."

At that moment, Henry knew it was over, even if his dad didn't. "That's not what I said, Jane. I said that in three or four decades, human technology might be employed as a weapon of war. It's entirely different."

"I don't care, Jacob. Take it back."

She spoke in a clear, steely voice Henry had never heard before. He knew her brook-no-argument tone from the salon because she used it all the time with beautybots, difficult clients and him. But this tone was completely hard and left no room at all for discussion. The conversation was over. Shut the file.

His father heard the difference too and snapped on his fan in frustration. "I don't even know whom to take it back to. Mr. Erickson's gone."

"Then keep it in your office until he returns."

"No, I mean he's gone gone," his dad said. "He left the day after I talked to Nickelby. I went to his office to brief him on the development, and his secretary said he'd retired. He cleared out his stuff and left. I've worked for him for 15 years and he didn't say a word, not even 'it's been nice knowing you, Jacobson.' All of the swatters were hurt. He didn't say good-bye to anyone."

Jane jumped on the information. "He's in on it," she announced.

"What?" Jacob asked.

"Erickson," she explained. "He's in on it."

"On *what*? he asked, his confusion meter set to COMPLETELY CONFUSED.

"I don't know. The conspiracy. The secret weapon. Whatever the mission for the human is," she said.

Jacob shook his head, flabbergasted. "Jane, close your story-telling app and think about what you're saying."

She ignored him completely. "We didn't want it, remember? We said we didn't want it, and the Motherboard made us take it. Something nefarious is going on," she said. "And Erickson is in on it."

"Jane, you're not making any sense."

"No, I am. Listen, Jacob, I'm a Zolot 5.0 managerial model, so I can tell you without question that no managerial model with his protocols in order would retire from his position without thanking his staff for their loyal years of service or accepting a gold-plated compass from his employer."

Jacob admitted she had a point there. Erickson's leaving *was* highly irregular. "But there could be a variety of explanations for that."

"No," Jane insisted. "There's only one explanation and now it's up to us to protect our son and our community. None of us are safe as long as that thing is walking the street. We have to destroy it immediately."

"Destroy it?!" Jacob asked, shocked. A minute ago they were talking about bringing it back to the office and now they had jumped to compaction. "I can't do that."

"You can't *not* do that."

"But Mr. Nickelby expects me to—"

"Mr. Nickelby expects you to protect your son and your community. He knows more than anyone that the safety of our country comes first."

His father was silent for a long time. Henry counted

one full minute before Jacob said, "All right. We'll bring it to the compaction facility."

Jane's relief was evident. "Thank you, Jacob. Thank you. I know this seems drastic, but I promise I wouldn't ask if our son's life weren't at stake."

"I wish you wouldn't worry so much," he said. "Henry's fine."

"I can't help worrying. I know he's had thirteen upgrades, but he's still my little botty."

Even with his sound sensor turned up all the way, Henry missed what his father said next. Then his mom said, "I'll get the human unit. You wake up the sedanmobile."

Henry's wires surged in panic. They were taking E *now*!

"No, Jane, tomorrow's soon enough," Jacob said softly. "Henry is going to have a hard enough time integrating our behavior. Let's not do it in the middle of the night. He'll be fine. I promise you."

Henry didn't stay for his mother's response. Instead, he sprinted up the stairs as fast as he could. There wasn't a single second to lose. He had to get E out of the house and far, far away from Sodium Falls before morning.

To do that, he needed a plan.

Getting out of the house would be easy but then what? Where would they go? What would they do? Henry tried to make a list of places they could go. He didn't have friends, so that ruled out their houses. Relatives? He had no grandparents. His dad never had folks and his mom's had been fried in a boating accident. He *did* have an elderly aunt in Hafnium Heights. She always sent him a card with twenty credits on his upgrade day. Aunt Sadie would take them in.

Yeah, and seconds later she'd pick up the communicator and call Jane. Even if he somehow convinced her not to, she'd be sure to mention him during one of their weekly chats. Besides, Aunt Sadie was the only family he had, except for a few weird, distant cousins he barely knew, so his parents would look there first.

Well, there was no point in worrying about it now. Sooner or later, he'd figure it out and until then he'd make it up as he went along.

E was waiting in Henry's room, scanning the latest MegaBot comic, "MegaBot #274: MegaBot Versus Red Menace." Henry himself was only halfway through it. MegaBot had been infected with a virus that was oxidizing his entire frame. In a matter of hours, he would be completely rusted out.

"I don't get it," E said as he flipped the page. "Hollister Holden looks the same with his HH amulet and without. How come no one notices he's MegaBot? Does the amulet have special vision-clouding powers?"

It was a question any fifth-upgrader who scanned comics asked at some point and one he himself had spent thirteen hours, forty minutes and eight seconds processing it, but Henry didn't have time to discuss it now. He snatched the comic from E's grasp and tossed it on the floor. "We've gotta go," he said abruptly, grabbing his school bag and throwing stuff—an extra fannypack, a travel-size capacitator, premoistened sparkle sponges, all the money he had. He took a box of CoalSnaps from the studystation's top drawer and caught a brief glimpse of his mom's knitted circus of clownbots.

He turned away, then looked back, then turned away again. Then he spun around, grabbed the juggler and tossed it into his bag.

E jumped to his feet, pulling a stuffed backpack from under the bed. "OK."

Henry couldn't have been more surprised if his friend had suddenly grown a gleaming alloy coat. "You're packed?"

E shrugged. "I figured this was a possibility. I knew your mother wanted to send me back and I knew I didn't want to be sent."

This kind of logic was supposed to be beyond a human's ability, but Henry didn't even notice. He already knew E was beyond human. "Good," he said, pushing his own knapsack higher on his shoulder, "let's go."

E didn't move. "You're staying here."

Henry swung around. "What? No."

"They won't come after me if you stay," E explained. "They just want me gone. They don't care how I go."

"No, now it's a matter of public good. Mom's convinced you're too dangerous to be walking the streets."

Even if it weren't a matter of saving E, Henry knew he couldn't let him go alone. A human on his own would stand out. Humans never went anywhere by themselves. Plus, E's photo had run in the daily download that morning. Everybot knew what he looked like.

"Then you have to stay and mislead them," E said. "Give me time to get away."

Henry dismissed this rationale too. He knew what E was trying to do. But he wouldn't let E risk his life so he could stay there in his cool, comfortable home. How could he possibly play video games or MARFELs or scan comic books when his friend was somewhere in the dark struggling to survive? Besides, he couldn't play MARFELs by himself.

"No chance. I'm in," he said brusquely, putting an end to the discussion. They didn't have *time* for this. Every second wasted arguing was a second lost. He wanted to be miles away before his mom came up to say good night.

Realizing they had to make their move, Henry glanced out the window on the side of the house—the front one would be too obvious—and considered the drop to the ground. It wasn't that far. They were only one story up. He could jump no problem. The shock absorbers in his joints would easily handle the landing. But he wasn't so sure about E. The human frame was laughably fragile. Everything harmed it. A fall from a *first*-floor window could break it. Then they'd have to call his service provider and *that* would totally ruin their getaway.

But it wasn't as though they had a lot of options. They couldn't just walk out the front door like they were taking an evening stroll.

Henry opened the window and felt the night air blow in. Then he turned to explain the plan to E, but his friend wasn't done making his case for a solo flight.

"Look," E said, "you've got a great home and a great family. Your mom's flipping now, but she'll get over it. It's a lot to give up. You can't do that for me."

"Yes, I can," Henry said gravely. He knew exactly what he was giving up, and it really wasn't that much—folks who didn't trust him, classmates who taunted him, a town that didn't understand him. No, it wasn't much at all.

But even if it was everything in the world, it wouldn't matter. When a friend needed your help, you gave it. That was the protocol. And he should know—he'd waited his whole life to have a friend to follow it for. "But I'm doing it for me too. I've been trying to bust out of this joint for years. Sodium Falls is b-e-n-u-m-b-i-n-g. Benumbing. Or haven't you noticed? So how do you feel about heights? Acrophobic?"

"Acro—what?" E asked, completely baffled. It was the first time Henry had seen him at a loss.

"Acrophobic," he said again with a grin. "Afraid of heights. From the Near Northern *acro* meaning 'topmost, extreme' and the Extreme Southern *phobia* meaning 'fear.' This window is our only way out. Do you want to go first or should I?"

Precious seconds passed as E stared at him silently. Henry knew he wanted to keep arguing. Neither wanted the other to go, but it was beyond their control now. Henry had to make sure his friend was safe. E knew that.

Finally, E shook his head, walked to the window and looked down. He stared out consideringly, then raised a leg and slid it over the ledge. "Acro?" he asked. "Seriously? That's the best you could do?"

Henry felt the warm glow of happy circuits. "I was under pressure."

E lifted his other leg. "I would have gone with heahphobia, from the Farthest Southern *heah* meaning 'high.'"

"Well, it's easy when you have time to think about it."

"Hey, that was off the top of my head. I guess some operating systems run better under pressure."

Henry rolled his sight sensors. "Whatever."

"Whatever," E repeated with a smile. Then he reached for the stalagmite tree formation near the window and shimmied down. "See you at the bottom."

Henry watched in amazement. It was the craziest thing he'd ever seen. Shimmying down a tree! Who knew that was even possible?

Henry shifted the backpack, climbed onto the ledge and looked down at E smiling confidently, his thumb raised in success. Then he glanced back at his room, his house, his life. It was a big thing, leaving home. He always thought he'd do it after his eighteenth upgrade when he went to university. He assumed his parents would stand on the doorstep and wave, his mother calling out advice like clean your coal capacitator after every meal up until the very last moment.

But now he was doing it ahead of schedule and without sage maternal wisdom. His mom had no idea that when she came up at ten-thirty to do the lights-out bed check that she'd find his bed empty.

He wished things could be different. He'd always gotten along fine with his folks. But this wasn't his fault. He wasn't the one who didn't trust her own son or believed the stupid lies of a stupid newsbot in a stupid daily download.

Resolute, he turned toward the window. It was time to make tracks. But as he pulled his other leg onto the ledge, the discarded MegaBot comic caught his sight sensor. It was opened to the page where Hollister first notices the rust. Two pages later, he realizes he'll be dead within hours if he doesn't capture and neutralize Red Menace. That was as far as Henry got.

On impulse, Henry jumped down and grabbed the MegaBot. It wasn't completely childish to scan comics. He knew plenty of adults who did. Besides, being on the run didn't mean literally running the whole time. They'd probably spend long stretches in hiding places with nothing to do. Having something to scan would be handy. Taking it was *totally* smart.

Comic book in hand, Henry jumped out of the window and into his new life.

CHAPTER THIRTEEN
ALCHEMIZED MITOSINATOR

Running away wasn't as easy as Henry thought it would be.

He assumed after jumping out of his bedroom window, they'd go straight to the Sodium Falls bus depot and hop on the first busmobile heading west. He'd always wanted to see the Very Far West and the Vast Open Space, where large herds of wild locomotives still roamed the land, but his parents hated going anywhere. They said robots who liked to sleep in strange beds and consume coal capacitated in unfamiliar capacitators had a glitch in their systems. His mom called it a travel bug.

E, however, had a plan of his own—take the first trainmobile to New Vanadium City and break into the Mainframe, the government agency responsible for defense.

At first Henry thought he didn't hear him correctly. Nobot in their right processor would want to break into the Mainframe. It was filled with scary G-bots who could shut down a system in a nanosecond. Federal Agency of Observation and Reportation agents didn't have to get a writ of disconnection. They could unplug you *whenever they wanted.*

It was terrifying.

"You don't understand," Henry said. "The Mainframe is in the Hexagon, a multi-storied, multi-shelled, multi-torture-chambered fortress. It's called the Hex cause it would take a magic spell to break in. And if you did get inside and they caught you, they'd throw you in the Pit."

He said the word *pit* softly like it was a curse.

And in many ways it was. The Pit was actually the United Territories of Greater Vanadium Proportional Correctional Facility, a federal prison reserved for the worst thugbots and villains in the country. A sweltering, pitch-black hole five stories beneath the Hex, the Pit was modeled after the most horrible coal mine in the history of the world: the Pit of Despair in the Extreme South. When it caved in sixty years ago, twenty-four robots were crushed to death.

Henry didn't know anyone who had been in the Pit, but it figured prominently in video games and comic books, so he knew it was horrendous. It was so hot down there the guards had special upgraded supercharged ventilation systems to combat the heat.

He tried to explain this to E, but his friend didn't care. "I get it. The Hex is impenetrable, and the Pit is a ditch of desolation. But I still have to do this," he said.

E leaned against the side of an old farm shed and squinted at the sun. After the aborted trip to the bus depot, they'd spent the night in the dilapidated building. To the north was a field of consolis, sleek rods on tall stalks, and rows upon rows of video-games-to-be danced in the wind. Soon, a farmbot would harvest the crop and bring it to a treatment factory to be turned into Melpitude CP-2000s.

Life, Henry realized, would be so much easier if it

were a video game. Then breaking into the Hex would be a grand adventure and if they failed, they could just press PLAY AGAIN. Mission Commander Scout Squad Mission to Save E from the World Commander Scout Jacobson reporting for duty, Commander, sir!

E pushed off the side of the shed and straightened his shoulders. "Look, I know you're worried. The odds are against my pulling this off."

Henry ran his probability app. "Against it? Try 1 in 234,589,002."

"So I can do this. It's not like it's completely impossible," E said with a smile.

Henry realized then that E was talking only of himself—*I* can do this, not *we*. He intended to break into the Hex all by himself. That was pure craziness. If Henry didn't know better, he'd say E had gone berserko.

But his friend was completely non-berserko and serious. He actually thought he could do it alone.

Now, that *was* impossible, Henry thought, running the odds on a solo trip into the Hex by a human. The numbers were off the charts. Clearly, he had to find the right line of reasoning to convince his friend not to do it. He opened his app for making clear and concise arguments. The first field said MODEL NUMBER. Henry put in E's ETC number. The application didn't recognize it, but Henry overrode it. Next it asked for the version of reality affirmulator E had.

Here, Henry didn't know what to enter. His knowledge of human internal architecture was limited. He didn't know if E had a reality affirmulator. Did humans even have a way of distinguishing real reality from fake reality?

Henry left the field blank and tried the override command, but the application wouldn't work without the vital piece of information.

"Here it is, bottom-lined," E said matter-of-factly. "I have to break into the Department of Security and Protection because it's the only way I'll ever know."

"Know *what?*" Henry asked, exasperated. He couldn't conceive of one byte of information that was worth dying for.

"What I am," E said.

Henry's sight sensors blinked in amazement. Had they really been arguing for an hour over something so simple? "You're an ETC-420-GX-2."

E expelled a loud breath of air. "I know, but what does that mean?"

"It means you're an ETC-420-GX-2," Henry said. E was an ETC-420-GX-2, just like Henry was a Zaklad 5000. It couldn't be any simpler: You are your model.

Circuitry is destiny.

What was so hard to understand?

E ran a hand through his hair and looked at the sky. "Just because I came in a box that said ETC-420-GX-2 doesn't mean I'm an ETC-420-GX-2. You read the article. Who made me? Where did I come from?"

Like most robots, Henry knew only the basics of human technology because the information wasn't included in standard upgrades. "You were made in a treatment factory in a machine called an alchemized mitosinator. The alchemized mitosinator exposes the synthesized protein matter to mitosis, which alchemizes it into a zygote unit. Then the zygote unit is put into a blastocystron, which adds important devices like the Cerebral Cortextinator and the Golgi Apparatus. Twelve days later, the zygote unit is removed and placed into the fetalisys, where the finishing touches like hair and nails are added. In all, it takes about two months to build each human unit."

While Henry spoke, E silently examined the sky. Slowly, he lowered his head and said, "My first memory is of a bright green light so blinding I couldn't tell if my eyes were open or closed. Then I was in a small room on a cold table and a robot was poking me with sticks that I later realized were his fingers. He never spoke to me, but during the examinations he constantly talked to himself as he recorded results. This continued every day for five weeks until I finally asked him to stop. The tests hurt. The robot was shocked. He hadn't initiated my language function yet, so he didn't think I could talk.

"Once he knew I could speak, he asked me hundreds of questions about what things looked and felt like. These interviews, which went on for hours, gradually became conversations. After a while, he taught me how to scan. He was away for long stretches of time, and he knew I needed to do something to keep my cerebral cortextinator functioning properly. I scanned everything I could get my hands on—books, magazines, instruction manuals, dictionaries. That's how I know so much. I spent eight months reading. It was all I did. From my reading, I knew what the world was like but I'd never seen it. So I asked the robot if I could go outside and he took me to a field with a lake."

E tilted his eyes up again. "I couldn't get over the beauty of the sky. Nothing I had scanned explained how it could make you feel surrounded by it or the way it could make you feel a sort of inner calm, like you had just woken up from a really good dream. It was hot out, so I jumped into the lake to cool off. The robot panicked at first, insisting that I get out immediately, but he saw that the water didn't hurt me and he let me splash around for a while.

"After that, the robot changed. He stopped talking to me and left me alone for days at a time. Two weeks later, he put me into the ETC box, said he was sorry and gave me a pink pill he called a storage tablet. The next thing I remember is waking up and seeing you."

E's eyes locked with Henry's sight sensors. "So I do know where I came—a green light and a cardboard box. And I do know who made me—a robot about the height of your dad with a bronze hue. But those aren't the answers. We both know I'm not a factory unit. My capabilities and functions are way beyond anything a standard-issue human can do. The robot or robots who built me never intended for me to sweep floors and botty-sit. They had another plan for me, and until I know what that is, until I know what I was built to do, I have no future and no present. I have nothing."

Henry knew what his friend was getting at, even if E couldn't actually say the words. "You're not a secret government weapon," he said firmly, his OddOdds processing the possibility. While it ran the numbers, Henry looked at the sky, trying to understand the concept of inner peace E had described. No such luck. Nor was he able to conceive of a light bright enough to penetrate his shuttered sight sensors.

No, he couldn't relate to his friend's experiences. But when E talked about needing to know the past to know the future, Henry's wires sizzled with understanding. Knowing your model was as basic as humming. It was the vital piece of information that made your operating system function. Without it, you had no protocols. Your reasonator would spin its wheels, unable to draw any conclusions.

Your thoughts would be a jumble.

No clear thoughts, no clear future.

Nothing.

Yet even without a reasonator to help him draw logical conclusions, E was capable of reasonable thought. Somehow, his ratiocination algorithms worked.

Surprised by this realization, Henry stared into his friend's eyes, as blue as the sky, and admitted that E was something special and new, a breed of human the world had never seen before. But he wasn't a force of destruction. Henry would bet his life on it, and by breaking into the Hex to prove it, he pretty much was. He had no choice. Henry understood that E needed answers and the Department of Security and Protection was the logical place to start.

"You're not a secret government weapon," Henry said again, his tone more forceful. "But let's go prove it."

CHAPTER FOURTEEN
HMT ACTION SUITS: FOR THE HUMAN
WHO HAS STUFF TO DO

Capitol Campus, the thirty-acre base of the federated democracy of the United Territories of Greater Vanadium located in downtown New Vanadium City, was larger than Henry remembered. The last time he came was two years ago with his dad on Bring Your 2.0 to Work Day.

Then it seemed like an upscale shopping center in Sodium Falls.

Today it seemed like a humongous government compound crawling with G-bots.

The campus was made up of three structures: the Triangle, which housed the Motherboard; the Polygon, home to the Circuit Tree; and the Hex. All three had the same gleaming white marble and imposing entrance columns, but only the Hex looked like a prison, thanks to the thick black bars on the windows. The buildings were separated by wide fields of gold-tinged topaz bordered by softly ticking digitalis, which when harvested and treated became timepieces.

"Here you will see the same ornate touches as elsewhere," the guide said, her voice modulator set to a steady I HAVE MUCH TO TEACH YOU SO PLEASE STOP FIDDLING WITH YOUR FANNYPACK. "Note the grand entranceway, the bas-relief panels, the elaborate balustrades, the gilded mascarons."

Examining the large empty space of the Hex lobby, Henry leaned over to E and said, "I have no idea what she's talking about."

"See those gold sculpted faces over the entrance?" E asked, pointing. "Those are mascarons. And above the——"

"Hay, stop that." Henry batted E's hand and looked around to see if anyone noticed. All the bots were listening with quiet fascination to the tour. They were in the clear.

Again.

But it had been a day of close calls. E stunk at being a regular human unit. Not only could he not stare fixedly into space with a blank, unfocused gaze, he continually pointed at things and made smart observations. Nobot would ever believe he was a regular human if he kept describing the mascarons.

E dropped his hand. "Sorry," he said softly. "I'll try to do better."

Henry could see his friend was making a genuine effort by squinting his eyes, but he still seemed far too interested in turn-of-the-century architecture.

"Drool," Henry said.

E looked thoroughly baffled, which, Henry noted with frustration, made him seem even smarter. "Let some saliva run out of the side of your mouth and down your chin. And stick out your tongue. A lot of human units do that."

His friend immediately obeyed, sticking his tongue straight out.

"No, no, your tongue shouldn't be stiff," Henry said. "Just let it hang limp."

E tried again.

Henry shook his head sadly. "Never mind."

"As you all know, the Hexagon houses the six departments of the Mainframe," the tour guide continued. "Shaped like a hexagon, it has six sides. Each of its six floors has six hexagon rings that are connected by twelve corridors. The rings, identified by letters, are called shells. The deeper you get into the building, the greater the security clearance. For that reason, we will be confining our tour to the E and F shells of the six departments. The first one we'll visit is the Department of Security and Protection, which ensures that every Vanadiumian is safe from enemies both foreign and domestic."

Finally, Henry thought. They'd joined the 1 o'clock Total Access Tour to get into the DSP but that was almost an hour ago. In the last fifty-three minutes and fifty-seven seconds they'd been subjected to one boring architecture lecture after another. It was like being in school but pointless. Why bother uploading info if you're not going to be tested on it later?

Smiling brightly, the guide led them through a large glass door that said STAFF ONLY and sweepingly gestured to the well-lit corridor lined with offices. The hallway had a low white ceiling, white walls and a speckled white linoleum floor.

Early-century extremely-not-so-cluttered, Henry thought.

"This is the F shell," the guide announced. "Here you will find staff with the lowest security clearance, and as you walk by, you might see some working at their desk. Feel free to wave hello."

Several of the group murmured excitedly, but as they walked down the hallways, all they saw were drawn blinds.

While the guide took them down another hallway, she ran through numbers: how many bots the DSP employed, how many worked in this building. Henry heard the information but didn't bother to process it. The only figure he was interested in was the likelihood that he and E could break into the department head's office, find E's file and get out of the building before G-bots shut them down.

Their guide stopped at a door marked 1F165, swung it open and told everyone to come inside. The office was square and gray with a desk along one wall and a couch against the other. A poster on the wall had one of his mother's favorite quotes from *Management Maxims for Maximum Success*: Winning is believing. "This is the command central of the DSP," she announced.

The tour group let out a general exclamation of surprise. The room was small, dingy and contained few items other than a file cabinet, communicator, disk receptacle, wall calendar and computer, a machine that stored, retrieved and processed data.

It was hardly the high-tech operation one would expect from the country's top spy department.

The tour guide smiled. "You're all looking around you, trying to figure out how a room so unimpressive could be command central of the DSP. It's sparse and low-tech. And that's exactly the point. There is no command central at the Department of Security and Protection. *Security* and *protection* mean that information can't be centralized. There are thousands of offices just like this one in the DSP and they all have the information the occupant needs to function and that's it."

While the bots around them murmured in appreciation, Henry met E's gaze and nodded. They knew what they were looking for would be in the department head's office—if it existed at all. Their logic was simple: Leader Mallory Cobaltstein was the top bot on the Security and Protect totem pole. If the government was developing a secret new weapon, she'd be in the know.

The tour continued to the E shell, where they were shown a conference room, another large, mostly empty space. A budget meeting was in progress, and for ten minutes Henry listened to moneybots argue about cash dispersal units. It was as microchip-numbing as a Yitteriumski tutorial on function integration, but the guide assured them they were getting a rare treat.

"Few visitors have an opportunity to see such important governance in progress," she gushed.

"Lucky us," Henry said softly.

E rolled his eyes and tilted his head meaningfully toward the door.

Henry got it immediately. With everyone intensely absorbed in the boring meeting, now was the time to make their escape. Slowly, he crossed to the door and peered into the hallway. It was bustling with activity. Robots in groups of two, three and four walked by, deep in conversation. Some were making a point or defending a decision. Others listened intently. Still others reviewed documents on the way to their destinations. All were wearing color-coordinated fannypacks to match their security clearance. In order of increasing importance, the colors were purple, blue, green, yellow, orange and red. None were black.

Henry, stepping into the hallway, was immediately swallowed by the sea of bureaubots. Without a file or the right-colored fannypack, he felt like an obvious imposter, but he kept his head up and his sight sensors alert. He glanced back quickly to make sure E was with him and almost stumbled when he spotted his friend carrying one leg of a table with four other humans.

Talk about an obvious imposter.

E stood out like a fried circuit. His jumpsuit was bright orange, his gait was straight and smooth and his eyes flickered with awareness. The DSP human units were slack-jawed and lumbering, their blank faces a sickly yellow against the pale blue of their jumpsuits. They appeared no different from most humans, but next to E's sharp intelligence they looked like they didn't have half a cortextinator between them.

Henry skipped over to where E was and pulled him away. The human let go of the table reluctantly.

"We're supposed to blend in," Henry whispered.

"I know," said E. "That's what I was doing. These are my people."

Henry shook his head. He didn't know what the term *people* meant, but now wasn't the time to make up words. "Stick with me."

The tide carried them to the B shell. There were several alloy-print-protected security points, which they passed through easily when the bot in front of them held the door open. This happened half a dozen times. The bots who worked in the DSP, a highly stressful, very demanding environment, didn't have time to acknowledge their coworkers, let alone notice a thirteeth-upgrader and his smart human friend. Only one swatter paid any attention to them at all and he merely looked at Henry and said, "On the fast track, eh?"

By the time they reached the B shell, the crowd had thinned out. Fewer bots had this level of security clearance, and those who did held important positions. They didn't have to scurry to answer to their boss because they were the boss. Therefore, Henry and E found themselves alone in a quiet corridor with an alloy-print-protected security point to pass through and no one to hold the door open for them.

"We could hide and wait for someone to come by, then run through before it closes," Henry suggested. "That's what MegaBot did."

"Where did he hide?" E asked.

Looking down the long, straight hallway, singularly lacking in nooks, crannies or alcoves, Henry tried to remember. "On the ceiling, I think." The superhero had SuperStickStuff on his touch sensors.

"I'd fall down."

"Me too," Henry admitted.

They fell silent again.

Henry knew they didn't have much time. Sooner or later someone would come down the hallway. E walked over to the alloy-print recognizator and raised his hand.

"Don't touch it," Henry ordered.

"Why not?"

"The alarm. The recognizator classifies and identifies all alloys. Yours will be unfamiliar and identified as an intruder."

"I'm not made of alloy," E pointed out. Then he ran a finger over the machine. No alarm sounded. "The recognizator needs an alloy print, but that's just to open the lock, right? The lock itself is an electric current. If we can break the current the door will open. All we need is something that doesn't conduct electricity, like plastic."

Although Henry had long since realized his friend was as smart as any robot, he was amazed again by his ability to reason. He'd taken a complex problem, broken it down to its components and solved it by using obscure information. Henry would never have thought of plastic. Why would he? It was only used to make botty toys.

But E had come up with it immediately.

"How do you know plastic doesn't conduct electricity?" Henry asked.

"No electric charges."

"Yeah, but how do you *know* that? I mean, how do you access information so quickly without a disk or hard drive?"

E shrugged. "I can remember everything I've ever scanned. The info is stored in my cortextinator, and it's there when I need it. I don't know how. It just is."

Henry found this idea incredible to process. In all the ways that mattered, a cerebral cortextinator was a simplified logic board. It could do some of the things a logic board could do, but it couldn't do them better and it certainly couldn't do things that a logic board could not.

Yet E's way of processing information seemed wholly different from Henry's. It was as if he could analyze data that didn't exist.

Henry tried to find a word to describe this unheard-of phenomenon, but there wasn't one in his dictionary. He spooled through a list of common roots and came up with a new word: imagination, from the Near Northern *imaginari*, meaning to "picture to oneself."

That was it, Henry realized: E had an imagination. By picturing data that didn't exist, he could produce solutions that weren't based on fact. Henry could not. His algorithms followed logic protocols, so the only solutions he could produce were logical ones. But with the ability to go beyond the limits of logic, E could take processing to new heights.

And just then, Henry got it. Finally, he got why his mother and the newsbot and all of Sodium Falls were so worried. Yes, E was different from other human units. Yes, he could process complex commands or reasonate complicated problems or even store huge amounts of data on his cortextinator. But that wasn't what had their worry meters set to MASSIVELY WORRIED. No, it was the fact that Henry could do *anything in the world*. He had no limitations. No boundaries. No restrictions. No restraints. No protocols. *He could do whatever he wanted.* Nothing was off-limits. Nothing was forbidden. His potential was endless. Given the right circumstances, E could do things Henry couldn't even begin to process. Things nobot could.

And that *was* terrifying.

"I know what you're thinking," E said suddenly.

Startled, Henry felt alarm surge through his circuits. The human knew what he was thinking? E could scan microchips too? Wouldn't that be a useful skill for a secret weapon?

His hazard meter initialized at VERY HAZARDOUS.

"You're thinking, But I don't carry around a piece of plastic for alloy-print-door-opening emergencies. Don't worry. I've got it covered," E said, reaching behind him and tugging on the collar of his orange suit. "These outfits come with a plastic tag. I've been meaning to take it out for weeks cause it itches like crazy." He pulled the label free with a loud tear and held the two-by-four-inch green card up for Henry. On the front side it said HMT ACTION SUITS: FOR THE HUMAN WHO HAS STUFF TO GET DONE. On the back were washing instructions. "Well, let's get this done."

E grinned as he lifted his hand to swipe the plastic

card, and Henry's hazard meter plummeted to UNHAZARDOUS. Of course his friend couldn't scan his microchip. And even if he could, it wouldn't make him dangerous. Henry might not know exactly what E was, but he knew for a fact he wasn't a threat.

No, the only threat here was of the little piece of seemingly harmless green plastic setting off every alarm in the Hex and flooding the hallway with G-bots.

Henry's OddOdds placed the likelihood of that happening at a relatively low 1 in 769,739, but the soft sound of his *wzzz-wzzz* whispered through his circuits anyway. Henry closed OddOdds and his hazard meter. He shut down everything he had, but the *wzzz-wzzz* continued to grow, which made his anxiety worse, which created more stress, which led to a more insistent *wzzz-wzzz*. Crash time was seconds away. It would strike right there in the B-shell of the most top-secret government facility in the world. He would be found lying on the floor when—

"We're in," E announced.

Henry looked up to see his friend standing in front of an open door. The *wzzz-wzzz* stopped.

"Now all we have to do is find the department head's office and search her files," E said as the door slid shut behind them, deflating Henry's excitement at infiltrating the A shell.

All they had to do—ha! The hard part was still before them.

E tugged his arm. "C'mon. We need a hiding place."

Henry knew this was true. In the empty hallway, they were completely exposed. There was no pretending to be an ordinary human or a fast-track prodigy now.

They didn't have far to go. Unlike the corridor in other sections, this stretch was short and ended at a silver door. Since their only options were to go forward or to go back, E matter-of-factly swiped his card. The door whirred and slid open.

E darted ahead, but Henry, standing on the threshold,

stared in awe at the room. It was massive, with a towering ceiling that soared six stories high. One entire wall was covered by a map of the Central Land Mass, with the Territories' neighboring countries, Very Far West and Extreme South, spiked with streams of light in a rainbow of colors. A thick red line slashed through the center of the capital of the Very Far West.

The adjacent wall had three gigantic television screens, each with an image so large Henry couldn't make it out. He was too close. But then he looked more carefully and realized it was actually the opposite; the screens projected hundreds of smaller images. Amazed, he stared at the countless scenes, trying to zero in on one, but his sight sensors couldn't focus with all the stimuli. For a split second, he thought he saw the intersection in front of the Shine Bar flash on the bottom right, but he knew he misread the image. All intersections looked alike. Besides, the Mainframe wouldn't care about his mother's beauty salon.

A heavy black data board covered the third wall, its cascade of constantly changing numbers and letters flickering blue. Like the monitors, this flood of information was impossible to take in. He had no idea what he was looking at.

But then he stepped back and took in the room as a whole and suddenly he knew exactly what he was seeing: the core of the Mainframe.

For sixty-two seconds, he stood there. It was like being in another universe. Like being in a video game instead of playing it. Like being part of the code.

Henry had always been taught in school that algorithms were the building blocks of life, but for the first time he *felt* it. It was impossible to stand there and not know with steady conviction that this was where he came from.

"Ferrous to Henry," E said, frantically waving his hands in front of Henry's sight sensors. "Come in, Henry."

Henry looked at him in surprise. "What's up?"

"What's up? What's up?" E asked in disgust. "You've been standing there completely spacing like a humbie, totally freaking me out, by the way, and you have the nerve to ask *me* what's up? We're about to get caught, that's what's up."

The *wzzz-wzzz* of fear buzzed and bit as Henry whipped his head around, expecting to see G-bots bearing down on them with leg-blurring speed. There was nobot there.

But he got the message. They needed to find cover. The massive room, filled with desks, tables, workstations and computers, offered plenty of places to hide. Henry pointed to a cluster of desks, and he and E just managed to duck under them before a pair of Mainframe officials brushed past.

It was a close call.

Too close as far as Henry was concerned.

"It's here," E whispered.

Henry nodded. This large, blinking, flickering, blue-tinged room was the pulsing logic board of the Mainframe. Anything worth knowing was here. They just had to find it.

The obvious place to start was with the computers. Although the Department of Security and Protection kept its computers separate, Henry strongly suspected that Mainframe central command was completely connected. The operation was too big not to have a networked information core.

E was clearly thinking the same thing because he crawled toward an unoccupied workstation across the aisle. Henry followed, his sound sensors turned to DETECT A BREEZE ON A MOUNTAIN TWO HUNDRED MILES AWAY. He heard a G-bot changing the setting on his stunnerator, dozens of swatters coding and E's even breathing. He heard nothing about intruders hiding under a cluster of desks.

Still, Henry left the relative safety of the cluster reluctantly. The workstation was only fifteen feet away but with the threat of capture looming darkly, the distance felt ten times as great.

E rubbed the side of the computer to wake it out of SLEEP mode. Henry hovered over his shoulder, impatient and excited. He couldn't believe he was here. Mainframe centcom. It didn't get better than this.

Or scarier.

The welcome screen blinked like the watchful sight sensor of a giant robot and asked for a password. Henry's impatience grew and his excitement dimmed as he realized he had no idea how to break into a network. Hacking protocols were a specialized skill and only included in professionally relevant upgrades.

But E was unfazed as he worked the computer's keyboard attachment. "I used to do this all the time during my captivity. The old bot had a computer that he'd often forget to put away. I liked playing with it. Once, I hacked into the municipal power grid and shut off all the lights for forty-eight seconds. That was a mistake. I was trying to unlock the door to my room and—"

He broke off abruptly and shoved Henry under the desk, kicking him with his feet to make sure he stayed down. Henry was too stunned to react and merely rubbed the spot where E's foot had connected. He had a new, small dent.

"Another creeper," a voice said.

From his disadvantaged vantage point, Henry could see two sets of legs. He inched forward to get a better look, but E kicked him again. He smothered an ouch and sank back.

"Flickering flameout! That's the fourth one this week," the other bot said. "What's it doing?"

"Typing the letter *d* over and over again."

"Maybe it's writing its name."

"Yeah, if it's name is Drool."

Both bots laughed. Then the first voice said, "Get it to compaction. You can use the wheelbarrow."

"Me?" he asked, appalled. "I brought up the last one. It's your turn."

"I brought up three last week."

"But I was on vacation."

The bots silently stood their ground while E continued to repeatedly type the letter *d*. Henry listened to the clicking of the control panel, panic setting in as he realized the danger his friend was in. Eventually, these dimbots, who seemed to be maintenance workers, not G-bots, would make a decision and one of them would dump E at the Hex's compaction facility. That would be fatal.

Henry had to do something, but even as he thought of shifting, E kicked him again. The message was clear: Stay put. Frustrated, Henry leaned back.

"I know, we'll have Charlie do it," the first bot suggested. His colleague instantly agreed, ending the standoff. Generously, they decided to bring the creeper to Charlie together. "Here, you get the feet. I'll get the arms."

The robot bent down to grab E's feet, his head dipping lower and lower until his sight sensors were almost level with Henry's. Henry tried to lean back, but he had no room to move. He was surrounded by desks on all sides. His hazard meter sparked to life, spitting out DEFINITELY HAZARDOUS. This was it. He was about to get caught.

Henry's bires wuzzed.

No, his wires buzzed.

Suddenly, a smothered squeaky sound followed by a noxious smell filled the small space and the bot quickly straightened. Everyone knew humans expelled a gross gaseous waste. It was a design flaw technologists had yet to fix.

"I'll get the other arm," the bot said.

The typing stopped abruptly as E was pulled to his feet. Free to move at last, Henry edged forward in time to see E being dragged away, his head lolling listlessly to the left, his tongue pressed between his lips. Finally, he looked like a regular human.

Not that it mattered now. Regular human or smart human, E was about to be compacted unless Henry could get to the facility and save him. He had no idea how he was going to do that, but clutching the plastic key card, he crawled to the door and hoped that the tide that carried him into the A shell would carry him out.

CHAPTER FIFTEEN
COMPACTION IS AS COMPACTION DOES

The Hex's compaction facility was on the second floor next to the mailroom. It was a large, sterile space with gleaming white walls, shiny white floors and bare, bright bulbs emitting streams of blinding white light. A clerkbot oversaw drop-offs at a long granite counter that ended in a conveyor belt powered by two dozen humans cranking handles. I COMPACT, ASK ME HOW was embroidered on his fannypack.

The facility was three times as large as the one in Sodium Falls but was set up the same way. A busted human was put on the conveyor belt, transported down the line and dumped into a compactor, which compressed it into a one-foot cube that was then safely deposited in a landfill.

By the time Henry arrived, E was already strapped to the conveyor belt. Finding the facility had been easy. The tour he and E had abandoned over an hour ago was still in progress. In fact, the group was exactly where they'd left it, in the E-shell conference room watching a budget meeting.

The guide had been happy to give him directions to the compaction facility, although she had been more than a little confused at how Henry could have lost his human. As far as she knew, the two of them had been there the entire time.

"Welcome to the Mainframe compaction facility, where compaction is as compaction does," the clerkbot said with a smile. "How can I meet your compaction needs today?"

With considerable effort, Henry tore his gaze from the conveyor belt carrying his friend to the compactor. "I'm here for my human."

The clerkbot reached under his counter, pulled out a pink form and placed it before Henry. "Fill out sections A, B, 4, Q, 9 and 35a of form HGJSL2," he said, marking the relevant areas with a blue highlighter. "We'll process your claim and get back to you in four to six weeks. Thank you and have a great day."

Henry's sight sensors flew to E. He was halfway to the top.

"But he, um, *it* is already on the conveyor belt. The ETC-420-GX-2."

The clerkbot's smile dimmed. "Oh."

"Oh?" Henry asked, his temper rising even as his emotionality stabilizer indentified anger and soothed it to mild annoyance.

"That's an HFPLV3S7."

Henry ran the code through his form-deciphering app and came up blank. "A what?"

"An HFPLV3S7. A human found in the A shell. Humans are not allowed in the A shell, and any human found in the A shell is slotted for immediate compaction. Thank you for stopping by and have a great day."

"No!" Henry yelled as E inched toward the top.

The clerkbot's bright smile returned. "Mainframe

compaction appreciates your feedback. If you have a question or comment, please fill out a comment card. Thank you and have a great day."

"But you can't destroy him, um, it! It's mine. I own it," Henry argued. "Possession is nine-tenths of the law."

"And the nonadmittance of humans in the A shell is the remaining one-tenth. Thank you and have a great day."

The clerkbot was clearly done with him, but Henry wasn't going anywhere. E was four humans away from being boxed. He had to do something fast. Jump the counter? Overpower the entire staff? Beg?

"Please help me," he pleaded. "My parents will shut me down if I come home without him, um, it. They saved for years to buy it. Please, please, please."

With a brittle smile but a voice modulator persistently set to PERKY, PERKY, PERKY, the clerkbot said, "Any human found in the A shell is slotted for immediate compaction. No exceptions. Thank you and have a great day."

"Stop saying that!" Henry yelled.

Now E was three humans away.

"What's the trouble here?"

Henry knew that voice as well as his own and, amazed, appalled, astounded, he spun around, his green sight sensors glowing like supernovas. "Mission Commander Nickelby!" he gasped, saluting like he did in the video game.

Yet Another Seat of Law Herbert Nickelby smiled and returned the salute. "Mr. Nickelby is fine."

"Yes, sir. Of course. Mr. Mission Commander Nickelby, sir."

Henry knew he sounded like an idiot, but he couldn't help it. He was *talking* to Mission Commander Nickelby! A true hero! A real-life MegaBot! The bravest, smartest robot in the history of the world!

While Henry stared at him worshipfully, Nickelby turned to the clerkbot and said, "What seems to be the problem?"

"He's trying to claim an HFPLV3S7. Per standard

operating procedure, all HFPLV3S7s are slotted for immediate compaction."

The clerkbot's explanation shook Henry out of his stupor and his gaze raced to E. He was one human away.

"But he's mine, Mission Commander, sir, and my parents spent a lot of money on him—I mean, it. They'll shut me down if I come home without it, I just know they will. My life will be over. Please help me."

E was next.

Nickelby took pity on the frantic boy and smiled at the clerkbot. "I think we can let him have this one, don't you?"

The clerkbot's expression made it clear that thinking had nothing to do with his job. "Per standard operating procedure YG7HB782+, all HFPLV3S7s are to be compacted immediately. No exceptions."

Unfazed, Nickelby said, "Still, I believe we can make an exception to the no-exception rule. Let him have his human back. I'm sure he'll promise to never let it wander into the A shell ever again, isn't that right?"

Henry couldn't believe his sound sensors. A reprieve! And just as E's feet were dangling over the edge! He grabbed Nickelby's hand and shook it enthusiastically. "Yes, yes, I absolutely double, triple, quadruple swear that my human will never, ever go near the A shell again. It'll never even enter the F shell. Thank you, sir. Oh, thank you."

The clerkbot pulled a lever and the conveyor belt stopped. He pushed it in the opposite direction and the dozens of Labor units cranked their handles counterclockwise. Slowly but surely E was being returned to him.

Although Henry had won, the clerkbot wasn't quite done yet. He fanned out six green-colored forms in front of Nickelby. "Per standard operating procedure, please fill out form YMSGPHAW1f stating that you ordered an exception to the no-execption rule. Please also fill out form YMSGPHAW1g stating that you understand that by ordering an exception to the no-exception rule you are paving the way for further exceptions. Please also fill out form YMSGPHAW1h stating that you understand that by ordering an exception to the no-exception rule and paving the way for other exceptions you are responsible for the consequences of those other exceptions. Please also fill out form—"

Nickelby waved a hand. "All right. I'm happy to fill out as many forms as your standard operating procedure requires. Send them to my office."

The clerkbot was thoroughly disgruntled by these many breaks in protocol, but for the sake of his career he had to agree. Yet Another Seat Nickelby was a very important robot. Henry, however, was still no one, and the clerk made him fill out half a dozen forms too. Some of them he obviously invented on the spot because they were blank sheets of paper.

Nickelby waited patiently while Henry finished the paperwork, asking him questions about his visit to the Capitol Campus. Was it his first time there? What had he seen? Where were his parents?

Henry used his fibbing app to help him keep track of the answers he gave. Keeping the truth to himself practically shorted his system. I'm Jacob Jacobson's son, he wanted to yell. I'm working on the ETC with you! We're partners!

But he knew to admit the truth would be to risk E's life. His mother was right about one thing. Mission Commander Herbert Nickelby's integrity was ironclad. If he thought for one second that the human was a threat to the citizens he had sworn to protect, he'd destroy it himself in an instant.

So he told an elaborate story about visiting the capital with his parents. He ended every sentence with "mission commander, sir," even though Nickelby insisted it wasn't necessary, and recorded every moment of the remarkable experience.

Finally, the belt returned E to the counter and the clerkbot had Henry sign three more forms before handing him over. "Your human, sir," he said scornfully.

Henry examined E. Other than a big red stamp across his forehead that said RETURNED, his friend looked no worse for wear. Smiling brightly at the clerk, Henry chirped, "Thank you and have a great day."

The clerkbot growled.

In the hallway, Henry thanked Nickelby again and again. His hero had saved the day! Nickelby assured him he was glad to help. "I have some time until my next appointment. How would you like a private tour of the Hex?"

Henry assumed his sound sensors were malfunctioning. "Excuse me, Mission Commander, sir?"

"A private tour. An up-close look at how your government serves you. How does that sound?"

It sounded amazing beyond belief, but Henry just said, "Thank you, sir." It took all his self-control not to high-five E. He knew E was just as excited. As a Commander Scout, he'd earned twice as many "bravo, soldiers" than Henry.

Nickelby led them down a series of hallways, quizzing Henry on the federated democratic process. "How many votes does a law need to pass? What's the average time it takes a bill to become law? How frequently are Seats elected? Name the piece of legislation that requires that all upgrades must be approved by the government."

Luckily, the stuff was all Civics 101, and Henry easily accessed the answers. Still, he soaked up each "correct," "accurate" and "right you are" his hero gave him like it was the Vanadium Metal of Distinction.

E trailed two steps behind, his head drooping to the side, his tongue hanging out.

Henry was enjoying himself so much he didn't even notice where they were going and suddenly found himself in front of one of the big silver doors that led to the A shell. He stopped abruptly.

"Mission Commander, sir, that's the A shell," Henry stammered.

Nickelby pressed his alloy print against the readout and entered a code. The door slid open. Henry didn't move.

Was this a test? In *Mission Commander Scout Squad,* Commander Scouts were tested all the time on their morality protocols. If a scout did the right thing, he got bonus points and was bumped up to the next level. If a scout did the wrong thing, he lost points and was busted down a level.

He didn't know what to do. Finally he said, "Mission Commander, sir, I can't go in there. I quadruple swore that I would never let my human into the A shell again."

"And so you're not, scout," Nickelby said. "*I'm* letting it."

Henry thought the distinction was logical and eagerly stepped into the large room. E followed. "Thank you, Mission Commander, sir."

The massive space was no less impressive the second time around. In fact, it was doubly so in the presence of a national hero and important government official. Now Henry could study the room without fear of discovery and get close to the huge machines that ran it all. Nickelby explained everything, from the maps that showed troop movements in every other country in the world to the statistic maker that created theoretcial mathematical equations.

"And this is the lab where we do our most important technological research," Nickelby said, opening the door of a large, well-lit room with lots of equipment. On the two black counters in the center of the room were Bunsen burners and beakers, which he knew from twelfth-upgrade chemistry, but the big contraptions that lined the back wall were completely foreign. The one on the left was a six-foot-tall box with a swinging glass panel on one side and a nozzle on top with various holes as if to spray something. It stood next to a mirrored cube about half as tall, with a control panel that had dozens of dials, buttons and switches. On the right was the strangest looking instrument of them all—a humongous ball with alternating black and white panels. It too had a control board in front with typing keys and four rows of blinking red lights.

"Come in, come in," Nickelby said, stepping back to

let Henry and his human pass. "Don't be shy. Have a look around."

Henry examined the apparatuses, marveling at how odd they looked and resisting the urge to touch. He still couldn't believe he was there. With Mission Commander Nickelby! No one at school would believe it.

"What's this?" Henry asked, standing in front of a small, spare space behind a panel of glass. Inside was a chair, a hanging bulb and a cardboard box.

Pleased with the question, Nickelby strode over and pressed a button. The glass slid away. "Ah, yes, we call this our habitatus. It's for our prototypes. We're in the process of developing a smart human as a secret weapon."

At the words *smart human*, E stiffened and lifted his head but it was too late. Before he could react, Nickelby pushed him into the habitatus and closed the door. E pounded on the glass with his fist. Henry dove for the button, but Nickelby dropped him with a sweeping kick and laughed.

"Do you really have so little respect for your elected officials?" Nickelby asked as Henry struggled to his feet. "Do you really think we'd protect your fellow Vanadiumians so poorly that any old thirteenth-upgrader can walk in off the street and into the A shell? We've had our sight sensors on you from the moment you jumped out of your bedroom window. I know who you are, Henry Jacobson. Your father's report filled me in quite nicely on everything I needed to know. My team wanted to apprehend you the second you stepped on campus, but I preferred to discover the reason for your visit. Unfortunately, the sweepbots mistook the ETC-420-GX-2 for a creeper before we could learn more. No matter. Thanks to you, I now have in my possession human technology that's light-years ahead of anything my own team has developed, which is all that counts."

Two G-bots entered the lab, top-of-the-line stunnerators strapped to their sides. Nickelby acknowledged the tall, wide-shouldered agents with a brief nod. "Please forgive me for not showing you out. I have some experiments to do," he said, pressing another button on the habitatus. A gray mist filled the room. Slowly, E stopped pounding, then fell to the floor, his eyes closed. Nickelby opened the door. Tendrils of mist swirled and dissipated. Before he stepped into the room, he ordered, "Take him to the Pit."

"No!" Henry screamed. Or maybe just thought it. He couldn't tell. The *wzzz-wzzz* in his head was louder than anything he'd ever heard before. It scrambled his circuits. He wasn't even sure what was happening.

Mission Commander Herbert Nickelby a villian?

He couldn't process it.

And now they were bringing him to the Pit? *Him?* Henry Jacobson? Lank Hank? It had to be a mistake. Or a malfunction. Maybe his reality affirmulator really was on the fritz. Maybe he did have bent-reality syndrome like the doctor from the Rutherford said.

The G-bots clamped their hands to his arms and dragged him to the door. Henry shuttered his sight sensors. It's not real, he told himself as he was carried through the hallway and down five flights of stairs to the festering prison where the hot air swamped his frame. It's not real.

But when he felt the scorching tar under his feet, smelled the acrid scent of overcapacitated coal and heard the dirgelike clang of his prison cell, he knew that it was.

CHAPTER SIXTEEN
ARTICLES OF INTEGRATION THIS AND
ARTICLES OF INTERGRATION THAT

Time stood still in the Pit.

Henry's timekeeping program claimed he'd been there for forty-four hours, twenty-six minutes and five seconds but he knew it had been much longer—maybe weeks, possibly months. The sweltering heat made it impossible to tell. Most logic boards began to malfunction at 92 degrees. The prison was kept at a staggering...at a staggering....

Henry didn't know. His temperature app couldn't get a read on the hotness. It had to be in the high 90s. Maybe the low hundreds. He really couldn't tell.

His photoelectric amplifier had conked out, too, leaving him incapable of seeing in the dark, a condition that prevailed in the Pit.

Silence also prevailed. All Henry heard was the clanging of cages slamming shut and the occasional moan of an inmate brutally disturbed from his hot, dark, silent rest by an angry guardbot.

Henry wondered when they would come for him. He knew someone had to eventually. This was Vanadium. You couldn't just toss a thirteenth-upgrader into a hot, dark, dank cage and forget he existed. He had rights. A trial. A lawyer. A call to his parents. They'd studied it in Civics. It was called habeas corpulence or something like that.

He didn't bother trying to access the right name because he knew it didn't matter what he called it. Habeas corpulence or crapulous, he still wasn't getting it. He was going to spend the rest of his life in this tiny cell, rotting slowly from the inside, his wires shorting one after the other until he was empty. He'd never look at the blue sky again. Never scan MegaBot again. Never see his parents. Never get one up on Sissy O'Thalium.

Oh, what he wouldn't give to hear her call him Lank Hank in the jeering tone right now.

Because it hurt to recall the outside world that was lost to him now (his parents spending the rest of their days waiting for news, hoping against hope for his safe return…), he turned his thoughts inward. He sorted through the apps on his hard drive.

HelioHelper: identified trouble spots in your game and suggested fixes. ViewVid: reinvented every landscape as a desert, forest, city and mountain range. RainReader: counted the number of rain drops that have fallen on you in your life.

Henry heard the clang of his cage door opening but didn't bother to look up. The guardbot would leave the thick, chunky sludge that passed for food and go.

"I have a mission for you, Commander Scout," the guard said.

Only it wasn't the guard; it was Nickelby.

Henry didn't respond—not because he didn't have the energy, although that was certainly the case, but because he couldn't bear to look at his fallen hero. This bot who he had worshipped for years. He was everything Henry had ever wanted to be. His own father didn't even compare.

Now he knew the truth. The Great Vanadiumian hero who talked all the time about strong morality protocols had none. And yet knowing that, Henry still couldn't help hoping with every circuit in his being that this was just another Scout Squad test.

He was a fool.

"Henry, good fellow, I need a small favor," Nickelby said, stepping deeper into the gloomy cell. The door swung shut behind him with a withering clang. "The prototype isn't responding to my commands. It can only recite beauty treatments and their prices."

For the first time in forty-four hours, twenty-eight minutes and fifty-eight seconds, Henry's system sparked with life as he pictured E rattling off a list of Shine Bar specialties.

"I know it's capable of more," Nickelby continued. "I scanned your father's report, which was remarkably informative in more ways than one. If you'll share the operational codes, we can discuss a new arrangement. I'm a compassionate bot—just ask any one of my eighty-nine biobotographers—so it hurts me to see you like this. At the very least, turn on your photoelectric amplifier. I hate seeing you wallow in the darkness."

Yeah, compassionate, Henry thought, as the dank heat of the Pit continued its assault on his circuits. Even with his reasonator not working, he knew Nickelby would never let him go. Henry Jacobson wasn't getting out of the Pit alive.

Henry Jacobson wasn't getting out of the Pit at all.

"I see," Nickelby said when Henry didn't respond. "You're sticking with the Commander Scout code: Give up nothing. Bravo, soldier! You're a credit to the squad. I wish I could say that mattered, but the game teaches unrealistic standards of behavior that ultimately set you up for failure in the real world. See, I can't let you keep the knowledge to yourself because I need it to fulfill my plan. I'm sure you're curious to know what my plan is, and I'm happy to tell you, as I know I can rely on such an honorable Commander Scout such as yourself to keep my secret. But even if I couldn't, it wouldn't matter. There's nobot down here to tell anyway."

The jeering tone barely penetrated Henry's microchip. All he heard was confirmation of his worst fears. No, he wasn't getting out.

"It's very simple," Nickelby continued. "A revolution is at hand. The world needs shaking up, and I'm prepared to offer it the benefit of my vast experience. Yes, I know many other bots think they know best, but I really do. So my plan is simple: Overthrow the government using human technology. I wouldn't have to act so radically if my co-Seats were a little more amenable to dictatorship. Alas, they are not. But my friends at HueManTech have kindly agreed to help me achieve my goals. For years, we've been trying to develop a smart human to build an invincible army, but the technology remained elusive. Now, thanks to you, we finally have a prototype. To show my appreciation, I'll give you one more chance. Tell me how to operate the human unit and I'll leave you alone. Don't tell me how and I'll attach these two little cables to your hard drive and send two hundred amps coursing through your frame."

Henry's head shot up. Even in the semidarkness, he could make out the cables clearly. Six feet long and one inch thick, they were far from little, and Henry knew the damage they could do wasn't little either. A power surge could short his circuits, fry his logic board and overcharge his microprocessor. *And* it would hurt like heck. Henry was stung by a wild stingray once, and his hand had throbbed for weeks.

"Still mum? That's your prerogative, but I should warn you that extracting information from an unwilling source is the best part of my job. Usually, it's a lot of paperwork and meetings. It can be very boring, especially the discussions about what constitutes lawful behavior.

The other Seats are so hung up on the law. With them, it's always the Articles of Integration this and the Articles of Integration that. Is it any wonder I want to overthrow them?" he asked, clutching the cables. "All that is to say, I get a real charge out of interrogations."

Henry believed it. Of all the things Nickelby had said, he recognized this statement as the absolute truth. The traitorbot would enjoy torturing him.

He knew that should matter. No robot should ever suffer pain to protect a human. A human wasn't alive; it didn't pulse or process. It was a thing, like a cup of T, and to sacrifice himself to save the life of a cup of T was pointless because a cup of T didn't have a life to be saved.

But it didn't matter.

And not because E was his friend, rather than a lifeless object like T, although that was a huge part of it. But because he, Henry Jacobson—little Lanky Hanky—was all that stood between Nickelby and world domination. He had to remain strong to protect Mom and Dad and Aunt Sadie and his co-workers at the Shine Bar and even Sissy O'Thalium.

"Now I must get out of here before the heat begins to affect my system. Take some time to mull over my proposition. It's twelve hundred hours now. I'll be back at thirteen hundred for your answer." Nickelby laid the cables on the bench next to Henry. "I'll just leave these here to help you reach the right decision. It would be a shame if I had to use them. I have been known to employ excess voltage in my enthusiasm."

With that final threat, he clanged once on the door and a guardbot let him out. Henry watched, the *wzzz-wzzz* in his head slowly subsiding to a dull buzz as he tried to process Nickelby's villainy. How far back did it go? Had the traitorbot always been bent on ruling the world or was that a recent development? The fact that Nickelby was working with HueManTech led him to conclude that he had been plotting his revolution for a long time. It might even go back to the invention of the first human.

Who else was in on the plot? The head of DSP Mallory Cobaltstein? The G-bots? The warden of the Pit?

Or was Nickelby working alone?

It was impossible to say. All Henry knew was he had to escape before Nickelby returned to torture him.

Hay, great idea, he thought, helplessly clutching the bars of his cage. He was fifty feet below the Hex in the most secure prison in the world. Murderers, terrorists, thieves and hackers hadn't found a way out but he would—and in the next forty-eight minutes and twenty-seven minutes.

I'm doomed.

The *wzzz-wzzz* in his head picked up, and he struggled to keep it together. If he lost power now, it was game over. He had to stay alert and figure out a way to escape.

Henry grabbed a cable and envisioned lassoing Nickelby the way his mom had that berserko human. Eagerly, he raised the cable high into the air, twirled his arm and smacked himself in the sight sensor. Absorbing the pain, he acknowledged it was going to take time to master the skill. He still had forty-two minutes and nine seconds.

And then what? Even if he did somehow manage to overpower Nickelby with a jumper cable, that was only the first step. He still had to get past the guardbots, climb five stories out of the Pit and navigate shells A through F.

Wzzz-wzzz.

No, he thought, not now.

But as he lifted the cable over his head and promptly whacked his verbalizor, he wondered, *Why* not now? If he crashed now, he wouldn't feel the hundreds of amps surging through his frame. If he couldn't feel anything, maybe Nickelby wouldn't bother torturing him.

Wait.

Maybe Nickelby would see his still frame lying lifeless on the floor and assume he was dead. It was entirely possible. Whenever Henry's power cut out, his system stopped functioning, making him seem entirely dead.

And how unlikely would his death be? Robots had to die all the time in this despair pit. The heat made their systems weak, and the prolonged lack of visual stimulation made their chips glitchy. No one would be surprised that a thirteenth-upgrader emptied under the stress. The real surprise would be if he didn't.

Henry dropped the cable and focused on the *wzzz-wzzz*. A few seconds ago it had been a loud buzz in his head, but now it was a soft murmur. Frustrated, he shuttered his sight sensors and concentrated harder. The sound remained elusive. It was like an echo in a cave—the harder he tried to reach it, the more it retreated.

To sharpen his attention, he tried conjuring up an image of the sound. For years, he'd thought of the *wzzz-wzzz* as a zippy little microcopter zooming intrusively through his head, so he pulled up a picture of the common botty toy. He saw the black two-inch frame with one rotor on top and a smaller one attached to the tail fin. Its rotors spun so quickly their blades blurred, creating perfect, whirling circles.

Holding the image was difficult in the heat. His processor worked slowly, causing the microcopter to sputter and pop a few times. Once, it dipped and nearly stalled. But Henry stayed focused. He concentrated on the copter, making it the center of his energy, and the buzzing grew louder and louder.

His frame began to shake with the force of it, and the familiar rattle sent a spark of fear surging through his circuits. For years, he had fought to keep the darkness at bay, and now he was inviting it in. It seemed wrong.

But he was already in the darkness.

With renewed determination, Henry followed the microcopter in his head. When the rattle started again, he held his focus steady and didn't flinch. The buzz filled his entire frame, and all he heard was the steady *wzzz-wzzz* of his own circuits, the sound of his current flowing.

Then distantly he heard metal clanking. He heard Nickelby say, "Commander Scout, to attention!" He heard him order the guard to examine the prisoner. He heard the guard call for a medic.

Then he heard nothing at all.

CHAPTER SEVENTEEN
RECLAMATION BUILDS STRONG NATIONS

Henry rebooted slowly. His microprocessor came online first, then his sensors, then his reasonator and reality affirmulator. While his system loaded, he was accosted by the sound of an angry robot yelling. It was all noise, loud and piercing, and he tried to lower the volume receptor on his sound sensor. But he didn't have volume control function yet. He knew it would return soon, as would all his other functions, including his photoelectric amplifier. The temperature in the room was set to an optimal 72 degrees.

"No, no, no, I said series 5869p—*p*, you burnt wire, not *b*. Let me talk to your boss." Pause. Screech. Shriek. "Your boss, your manager, your supervisor, any swatter there with one day's seniority over you. I don't care who as long as they can fire you." Pause. Grunt. Growl. "No, I'm not kidding. I'm done with you. Get off the line now."

The room was bright, large and filled almost entirely with tall shelves containing neat groupings of frame parts—groups of arms, groups of hands, groups of logic boards, groups of legs. Across the room, on the other side of the shelves, was the angry female administrator. She sat at a desk piled high with folders, her frame hunched over, her back to Henry. On the wall above her calendar a sign said RECLAMATION BUILDS STRONG NATIONS.

Reading it, Henry knew where he was: the Pit's reclamation center, where they processed hardware donations. Dead robots were brought here so their parts could be reused. His plan had worked. Nickelby believed he was a goner and had him brought here to be chopped up.

Henry waited for his clock app to initialize. It was 2:32. He'd been out for one hour, twenty-eight minutes and forty-six seconds. Usually his crashes lasted ten to fifteen minutes. It must have been the unbearable heat that had kept him out for so long. And lucky thing too. Now he was free of Nickelby's clutches.

Well, he would be as soon as he escaped the Pit and the Hex.

To get started on a new plan, Henry carefully raised his head to see more of the room. Six tables lined the back wall, including his; two had empties on them (not including him). Cubbies leaned against the adjacent walls, each one labeled with the name of the employee it belonged to.

Across the room, the adminbot turned her voice modulator up to RAISE THE DEAD and reamed the swatter on the other end.

The doors opened and a pair of robots entered, clipboards in their grasps. Henry dropped his head back to the table and watched as the newcomers browsed the shelves, examining various frame parts. They snagged arms and left.

In the half hour that followed, many robots flew into

the room and breezed out, some to retrieve frame parts, others to return equipment, still others to get documents signed. Through all of this, the adminbot remained on the communicator, yelling at whomever was on the line. She never once looked up.

Watching, Henry decided the best way to escape was simply to get up and walk out. He could put on a white lab fannypack stamped with PROPERTY OF UTGVPCF RECLAMATION and stride through the door without anyone noticing. And the time to act was now while it was just him and the admin. Sliding off the table, he kept his sight sensors trained steadily on the ranting bot and dropped to his knees. He crawled five feet and stopped when the door opened again. Through the shelves, he saw two labbots walk past one row of shelves, then another and another and another until they were almost on top of him.

Oh, no!

In a panic, Henry threw his arms and legs out to the side and fell flat against the floor. He wasn't sure if he was trying to hide or play dead.

If he was trying to hide, it was a complete failure. The robots stopped so close to Henry he felt the air swirl around him. They were silent for a moment, then one said, "That's strange."

The other agreed.

Henry, his smell sensor pressed to the tiles, struggled not to move his head. The scent of purification fluid and stale coal was so strong it could short a wire.

"How do you suppose the empty got here?" the first one asked.

"Dunno," his colleague said. "Fell off the table?"

Henry was five feet four inches from the table. He didn't need his vector-measuring app to tell him it was impossible for an object his size to land five feet four inches from where it fell.

Maybe they wouldn't notice.

No such luck. "The table's five feet four inches away."

142

"I guess it rolled."

It was the dumbest explanation Henry had ever heard in his life. His circuits fired as he prepared for a fight. He wouldn't return meekly to his cage.

"Yeah, I guess it did."

"Should we move it back?"

"We can't just leave it lying here."

Henry kept his joints loose as the bots grabbed his arms and legs and heaved him to the table with a careless drop. He landed painfully on his left shoulder. Another new dent.

Back where he started, Henry waited for the robots to collect their hardware and leave. Then he implemented his plan again, jumping down and running to the cubbies. He put on the fannypack, stuck the name tag to his chest and picked up the clipboard. From the shelves, he snatched the first frame part he could reach—a head—slid it under his arm like a helioball and briskly carried it out of the room.

In the hallway, he didn't stop to get his bearings. He went right, then left, then right again, keeping his head down. Although no one in the busy hallway looked twice at him, he knew he didn't fit in. He was too short to be anything but an underage prisoner trying to escape after faking his own death.

Nickelby was probably watching him right now. He had surveillance cameras everywhere, and the last time Henry roamed freely through the Hex, thinking he was getting away with something, Nickelby had been following his every move.

Picking up speed, he took the next right, then a left. Suddenly, he was back in the deep, dark, stifling core of the Pit. The heat hit him like a wild truckmobile. He spun around to get out, but his reasonator, sizing up the situation, told him to stay the course. The darkness provided cover, the tunnels were less crowded, and his

143

way-finding app had charted some of the area on his way in. Through the Pit was the best way out of the Pit.

His photoelectric amplifier initializing and his way-finding app loading, Henry pushed ahead despite the soaring temperature. Like the original Pit of Despair, the prison was a maze of endless dark tunnels. He walked past cage after cage, seeing none of the other prisoners through the bars. They were all on their cots, staring blankly into the void.

Despair was an understatement, he thought, recalling the enervating feeling of being locked inside a cage. It was like the walls themselves sucked the energy from your circuits.

His way-finding app beeped, alerting him to familiar territory, and he stopped. The stairwell wasn't far from here. His own cage was down this tunnel and—

Out of the darkness, a voice called his name.

Henry felt terror, sheer stark terror. The terror was so intense it shocked his system, sending a surge of power so strong through his wires it left him weak. His stabilizer immediately kicked in to downgrade it to plain old manageable fear, but, already crippled by the heat, it got stuck at petrified.

"Henry," it said again.

It was impossible, Henry knew it was, but he felt as if the tunnel itself were calling his name, drawing him back to the coal-black walls of death where it knew he belonged.

"Henry," it seethed a third time.

Very slowly, Henry turned around. The cage in front of which he stood was occupied by a tall robot clutching his prison bars with both hands.

It was Mr. Erickson.

CHAPTER EIGHTEEN
THE MOST LIKELY FAKE BUT POSSIBLY REAL MR. ERICKSON

Henry knew he was seeing things.

His dad's nice, friendly boss wasn't locked up in the world's most notorious prison with murderers, thugs, thieves and terrorists. It was just a projection, an image from his hard drive wrongly projecting itself externally. His reality affirmulator should've picked up that it wasn't real, but it was probably malfunctioning like his emotionality stabilizer. If he didn't get out of the heat soon, his entire system would go down.

With no time to spare, he pivoted and began running, clutching the reclaimed head firmly to his side. The projection called his name again, its tone desperate and pleading.

That was weird, Henry thought. Projections didn't have audio files. They were just visuals. He stopped and spun around. The Mr. Erickson projection was holding out his hand. "Henry, you have to help me."

Henry reached for the hand, fully expecting his fingers to pass through empty space, and felt his touch sensors press against solid alloy. Something was there but what? It couldn't be Mr. Erickson. Maybe his reality affirmulator was reading one object as another.

If that were true, then he was grasping the hand of a murderer!

Henry let go and jumped back.

The robot, whoever he was, became more frantic. "Please, Henry, we need to hurry. Ethan is getting weaker by the minute."

Now Henry realized it was the prisoner's reality that was bent. Too many years locked away in the deep reaches of the desolate Pit had destroyed his microchip. He was a rambler.

But if he was just rambling, how did he know Henry's name? A lucky guess? Henry told himself it didn't matter. The bottom line was Henry didn't know any Ethans, and the only robot getting weaker by the minute was he. He *had* to move. But before he could, the imposter Mr. Erickson snatched his hand and clung to it like a RainRescueSlickGuard in a monsoon. "The ETC, Henry. You have to help me save him. I gave him to you to protect. We have to save him."

Shocked, Henry stopped struggling. "E?"

Suddenly, the most likely fake but possibly real Mr. Erickson froze and said, "Shh! The guard is coming. Hide!"

Henry's circuits sizzled in panic. Hide?! There was no place to hide! The Pit was a maze of dark tunnels punctuated with locked cages. Regardless, he ran deeper into the tunnel and pressed himself against the wall. Think invisible thoughts, he told himself, think invisible thoughts.

But he couldn't think at all. His system was overcome with pure terror that refused to be stabilized. The *wzzz-*

wzzz zipped through his head at deafening decibels. Frantically, he closed apps. Clock, way-finder, OddOdds.

WZZZ-WZZZ. WZZZ-WZZZ. WZZZWZZZWZZZ.

The sound was so loud Henry knew the guard in the tunnel could hear it. And not just him. All the guards in the Pit, even the ones napping in the break room. It was like an alarm alerting the entire Mainframe to an escaping prisoner. Any second now a whole squad of G-bots would descend on him with their war machines in tow.

War machines! Aircopters!

Henry shuttered his sight sensors and struggled to find the microcopter. His system was frazzled. He couldn't concentrate. He tried to remember where he filed the image, but his chip was blank. The pressure mangled his search function. He was going to crash.

No, stay calm. Don't lose it. You can do this.

He ordered himself to be methodical. He checked all his drives, one after the other, and suddenly there it was—a tiny flying machine making wild figure eights over mountains of pale yellow marcasite.

He had to quiet it down.

Quickly, Henry aimed the copter for the farthest hill. As the machine drew closer and closer to the horizon, the sound of its rotors dimmed. The energy surge dissipated. His thoughts cleared. The *wzzz-wzzz* softened to a murmur.

Yes! For the first time in his life, he actually controlled the disability. It was amazing.

"Ten-hut, Tinsmith!" the guardbot hollered over the clang of the cage. "The esteemed and much-respected Mr. Yet Another Seat Nickelby requests your presence."

"You can tell the unesteemed and much-reviled Mr. Yet Another Sleaze Nickelby that the prisoner denies his request."

Henry looked out cautiously from the gloom and saw the guard take a threatening step into the cell. "Your preference settings aren't my concern. The prototype unit is malfunctioning and your technical skill as its inventor is demanded."

Henry's processor whirred as it ran a search on the

keywords *Tinsmith, inventor, prototype* and immediately spit out Felix J. Tinsmith, human inventor.

Human inventor who *died* more than forty years ago!

But Henry didn't doubt the conclusion. Tinsmith was Mr. Erickson, who was his father's boss, who gave him the ETC to protect. And that meant Ethan was E, who was the prototype that was malfunctioning.

"Malfunctioning how?" Tinsmith asked.

"It's dripping sticky, red stuff," the guard said.

Knowing how dire dripping red stuff could be, Henry sprung into action. He charged forward, yelling "hay, you," and hurled the head he'd been holding at the guard. It struck between his sight sensors, stunning him. Henry tackled him to the ground, pounding him with clenched fists. The guard scissored his legs and flipped Henry, pummeling him. Stupefied, Henry stared unseeingly up as the bot landed on top of him with a grunt. Henry's frame collapsed under the weight. He flailed his arms and legs, kicking and swinging but couldn't break the hold. The guard pressed down harder and harder, increasing the force in small painful increments, and Henry knew his logic board was about to be crushed.

Then, just when Henry thought it was lights-out for good, the guardbot went limp. Feeling the sudden release of pressure, he heaved the guard off and saw Tinsmith kneeling beside him, the guard's stunnerator in his hand.

"Come on," Tinsmith said, pulling Henry to his feet. "Ethan's leaking."

Henry dragged the offline guard onto the cot, then ran out of the cage, slamming the door behind him. He followed Tinsmith through the tunnels to the stairwell, which Tinsmith opened with his alloy print.

Amazed, Henry stared as the door slid open. "How did you—"

Tinsmith pushed Henry through the opening. "Hurry. There's no time to lose." They took the stairs because

Tinsmith said it would be quicker. The elevators, powered by hundreds of humans, were slow and could take up to five minutes to come.

"I don't understand. Who are you?" Henry asked.

"Felix J. Tinsmith," he explained, climbing. "I invented the human forty years ago. I worked for HueManTech. Nickelby was my boss. Even back then he was relentless, never satisfied with anything. It was always, Work harder, Tinsmith, work faster. He said I was too distracted by my wife and infant son and suggested that he keep them in a safe place until I finished my project. After he threatened my family, I came up with a plan to fake my death and disappear."

They reached the fourth sublevel. Three more flights to go.

"My plan went disastrously wrong. After my supposed death, my wife, Martha, relocated. I waited for months for her to send word of where she was but it never came. I started searching. It took me a full year to discover what happened, but I finally learned she'd been killed." He paused a moment, his sight sensors shuttered briefly as he mounted the next step. "It was a random act of violence. They never found who did it. By then my son was gone."

They were at the third sublevel now.

"They put my boy in an orphanage and wouldn't let me have him because I couldn't prove I was his father. I tried to adopt him, but they suspected my motives and rejected my application. After that, they wouldn't let me near him. With nothing left, I returned to my work with humans, toiling in a secret basement lab nobody knew existed. But at the same time I knew it was vitally important that I keep my sight sensors on Nickelby, so I disguised myself and signed on as a swatter in the Circuit Tree. I rose quickly through the ranks. Years later, I met my son again and offered him a job. Ah, how bittersweet—to see my darling boy every day and be a near-stranger to him." After a moment of silence he continued. "Somehow I knew

Nickelby would find me again, which he did in the end, though I have no idea how. So to protect myself I hacked into the system and put my alloy prints on file with the highest clearance. I never actually supposed I'd need it to break out of the Pit, but now that it's happening I'm not that surprised, for I always knew Nickelby was a villain."

They flew across the second sublevel landing. Almost there.

"For four decades I worked on my invention. I scrapped dozens of units, but with each one I made some small improvement on the cerebral cortextinator. My last design you know as the ETC-420-GX-2. I realized immediately he was different. He could acquire language. He could scan. He could process independently and reasonate. He had perfect recall for details. He was smart, so much smarter than even myself. And so curious about the world. I took him outside once, and we came upon a lake. He jumped right in, and while I was watching him splash around unharmed by full immersion in water, I realized that the Robothood of Peace had been right all along. In the wrong hands, this human could be a weapon of war. Build hundreds, thousands, millions more, and they'd be an unstoppable army. But knowing the danger, I couldn't just scrap him like I had all the others. Ethan was alive. Every breath he drew carried air to his lungs and brought oxygen to his remarkable cortextinator, where millions of synapses fired millions of little electrochemical waves. No, I couldn't possibly scrap all that. So I boxed him up in a regular ETC carton I picked up at a HueMart and I gave him to my son for safekeeping."

Tinsmith reached the top step and pressed his hand to the door for a print scan. Behind him, Henry stumbled on the last step. "But...but..." he said, stumbling on the words too. He replayed the last sentence. *I gave him to my son.* If Tinsmith gave E to Henry's dad and E was given to Tinsmith's son that meant Tinsmith was—

"I'm your grandfather, Henry," the inventor said gently.

CHAPTER NINETEEN
MISSION TO SAVE THE WORLD

Staggered, Henry stared at Tinsmith—*his grandfather?!*—and struggled to process the idea that his dad had a dad. It seemed completely illogical that Jacob Jacobson was Felix J. Tinsmith's long-lost son.

"But I don't—"

Tinsmith raised a finger to his verbalizor to indicate total silence and slipped through the door. Henry followed, his reasonator registering the new development as COMPLETELY UN-ILLOGICAL. The facts of the story fit Jacob's life. His mother *had* been killed in a random act of violence. He *had* been raised in an orphanage. Mr. Erickson *had* appeared out of nowhere to give him a secure government job.

It was so microchip-blowing, Henry didn't pay attention to where they were going. Suddenly, he was outside the door of Nickelby's lab and Tinsmith was telling him to rescue E. "I'll make a distraction," Tinsmith announced before stalking into the room. He was gone before Henry could ask him *how* he was supposed to rescue E.

"What have you done now, Nickelby?" Tinsmith asked, his voice modulator turned to I HAVE MUCH MORE IMPORTANT THINGS TO DO. The impatience in his tone made it seem like he hadn't faked his death forty years ago and still worked for the tyrannical HueManTech executive. "I did exactly what you asked. I built the world's first smart human, per your specifications. I did it on time and within budget and then the first chance you get you go and break it."

Nickelby's sight sensors were trained on the inventor as he marched over to E, who was strapped to a table, and Henry slipped into the room. He hid behind a tall shelf stocked with human supplies and watched through bottles of Go-Go Pep Solution.

Across the room, Tinsmith examined E and tsk-tsked with disapproval. "This time you've really done it. Congratulations, Nickelby. Your talent for destruction is unsurpassed. Give me that S-clamp," he ordered.

To Henry's surprise, Nickelby actually did, handing over the small round tool.

"No, not Q-clamp, the S-clamp. That one." Tinsmith pointed impatiently at a long, thin clamp. "You've busted the sinus tab and the cortextinator is leaking out of the nose cavity. I can stem the flow, but that's just a temporary fix. I have to repair the tab. Start the mitosinator. It must be re-metastasized immediately. Quick, there's no time to lose."

Nickelby jumped to do his bidding, and Tinsmith waved a hand behind his back. Henry knew this was his signal. Somehow he had to free E and get him out of the room and the Hex without Nickelby or anyone else noticing. He didn't have any idea how to pull it off but now wasn't the time for ideas. Now was the time for action.

Henry straightened his shoulders. Before he could do more, Nickelby stopped, and in the split second before the commander turned around, Henry knew he knew. The villain's reasonator had analyzed the whole scene and realized something was wrong. Tinsmith was here but where was the guardbot?

The inventor also knew Nickelby knew, but he tried to brazen it out. "What are you waiting for?" he demanded. "I've worked my whole life to build this unit, and you're destroying it with your carelessness." He pulled out the guard's stunnerator and aimed.

Nickelby laughed and in one smooth, swift motion disarmed the inventor. "You turn it on, doctor," he said, picking up Tinsmith and throwing him at the alchemized mitosinator. He crashed into the machine's glass door, breaking it into a thousand little pieces, and landed on the floor with a clunk. The mitosinator whirred to life, glowing a bright green.

"Now, your ally," Nickelby announced. "Come out, come out, wherever you are."

Hidden behind the shelf, Henry knew it was only a matter of time before the Mission Commander threw him against a machine too. He didn't bother to wonder how Nickelby knew he was here. The Metal of Distinction winner's hero drive was well honed from years of brave and daring exploits.

Working with what he had, Henry picked up a bottle of Pep Solution and hurled it at Nickelby. It flew through the air, flipped once, then twice, and landed an inch short of its target. Keeping his head down, Henry threw another bottle and another bottle and another bottle and another, tossing them across the room one after the other in rapid succession. Each shattered on the floor.

"Is that you, Commander Scout, risen from the dead?" Nickelby called. "Bravo, soldier. Evading the enemy by faking your death is a classic maneuver. Two thousand points for good execution."

In throwing the bottles, Henry had given away his position. It was a necessary risk, but now Nickelby was walking straight toward him. The Mission Commander was in no rush. He had Henry cornered.

"But I'm sadly disappointed in your combat skills," he added. "Throwing projectiles willy-nilly at the enemy isn't a well-conceived battle plan. Where's your battle plan, soldier?"

Henry had to move. The shelf was long and provided enough cover for him to get to the far wall. But Nickelby was right; he needed a plan. He looked around. All he had was the stuff on the shelf: 34 bottles of Go-Go Pep Solution, 10 jumpsuits, 4 pairs of shoes, 60 PoopPouf waste-treatment kits, 2,000 MARFEL pellets.

"If there's one thing I've taught you it's never enter a battle without a plan," Nickelby said, drawing closer. "It's basic Scout Squad training, Commander Scout. For that, I'm afraid I'm going to have to deduct 5,000 points."

Working quickly, Henry pulled down two jumpsuits. He put one on and stuffed the many pockets with solution. He tore the second in half and in half again until it was a square. He emptied the pellets onto the scrap of cloth and folded it up so that the MARFELs wouldn't spill out until airborne. Then he crept to the end of the shelf. Nickelby was three feet away.

It was now or never.

With all his force, Henry heaved the jumpsuit high into the air. The makeshift bag opened and rained hundreds of MARFELs onto the floor.

Nickelby laughed scornfully. "You really should know better, Commander Scout," he said before he fired Tinsmith's stunnerator as well as his own. Two steady streams of purple light streaked toward Henry, then darted to the ceiling when Nickelby slipped on the MARFELs. As he wobbled precariously, Henry carefully lined up his shot and threw a bottle. It hit Nickelby square in the chest.

Score!

Purple stunnerator beams flew everywhere—at the

walls, machines, tables, jars, floor. Dodging rays, Henry aimed for Nickelby's sight sensors. He missed! The bottle smashed on the floor. Henry threw another and connected with Nickelby's left hand. The stunnerator went flying.

Henry dove for it, abandoning cover for the open field. He landed three inches short. He scooted forward, stretched his arm…. Almost…almost….

Less than two feet away, Nickelby bobbed back and forth on the MARFELs. He held out his arms for balance but fell backward, his frame clanking to the floor. He raised his legs and used the leverage to flip over just as Henry gripped the stunnerator.

"Aha!" Henry cried triumphantly. He aimed the stunnerator at Nickelby and pressed the—

The small device flew from Henry's hand, skidding across the floor. Shocked, he stared at his fingers sizzling and tingling from the blast. He looked at Nickelby towering over him, the evil grin of victory spreading across his evil face, the other stunnerator grasped expertly in his left hand. "Rookie mistake, Commander Scout," he said. "Never give up your cover. How many times have I told you to keep to the underbrush. You lose points again."

Henry knew a stunnerator set to APOCALYPTIC ANNILIATION was a thousand times more powerful than any electroshock treatment. One blast could empty a robot of all life in 0.7 seconds. But he didn't turn away or shutter his sight sensors. He didn't feel fear, only regret. Nickelby had won. He would torture Tinsmith. He would destroy E. He would wage his war for world domination.

And there was nothing Henry could do to stop it.

His mortal enemy's smile grew wider. He was thinking exactly the same thing. "Game over, Commander Scout," he said, then pressed the button.

Henry didn't flinch. It would be over before it even started.

But it didn't start.

He looked at Nickelby's fingers. They weren't moving. His hand was still!

155

Amplified ampage! The Go-Go Pep Solution had shorted the wires. Nickelby's hand was dead. And the well-seasoned commander hadn't realized it yet! His microchip couldn't process his motionless fingers.

Henry saw his opening and took the last bottle of solution. He threw it straight at Nickelby's head. The former hero looked up just in time to see the bottle crash into his smell sensor. Hydration fluid ran everywhere, filling his sight sensors, spilling into his verbalizor, saturating his logic board, soaking his microprocessor.

Sparks flew, first out of his sound sensors, then out of his verbalizor. His system sizzled. His wires crackled. Swirls of smoke twirled from his sound sensors. He bent his head forward, sight sensors glued to his unmoving hand. Then, astonishment on his face, he dropped to his knees and fell backward. His frame hissed, spit, sputtered and died.

"Game over, Mission Commander," Henry said as Pep Solution dripped onto the floor. Then he rushed over to where his grandfather lay. The old inventor's sight sensors were shuttered, but Henry could hear the faint hum of his fan. He was alive! Henry patted him on the chest. "Wake up, wake up. Please wake up."

Tinsmith only grunted.

Henry raced to E. His friend's face was as white as the walls, and a trail of red ran down his cheek. His cortextinator! It was leaking out of his nose. The sinus tab needed to be re-metastasized immediately or he would die. Knowing nothing about the process, he carried E to the green-glowing machine. He started to put him inside, ignoring the glass that would cut the human's soft alloy.

"Whoa," Tinsmith said, standing up. He teetered back, then regained his balance, "not the recommended treatment."

"But his cortextinator—"

"Just a leaky nose," he said brusquely. "Press a fabric square over his nostrils and he'll be fine. Now let's get you home. Your parents must be worried."

156

The journey out of the building was much like the journey in. They moved quickly and anonymously through the busy halls. Tinsmith's alloy print opened every door and no one bothered them. E woke up in the C-shell and Henry stopped to put him down, but Tinsmith pressed him on the back and said, "Keep moving." A malfunctioning human that had to be carried was a common sight; one that recovered enough to walk for itself was not.

They passed swiftly through the A-shell, then the B-shell, then the elaborate lobby. Then they were outside, on the steps of the Mainframe, the tall imposing building that housed a prison behind them, the sun overhead. They strolled purposefully along the path lined with digitalis swaying in the breeze and walked off the campus like they were regular tourists. No alarms sounded. The gates didn't come down. The guardbot hardly looked at them at all.

They kept going. One yard, two yards, a dozen, a hundred, a mile. Henry couldn't believe it. He was safe. E was safe. His grandfather was safe. The citizens of Vanadium were safe. Everyone was safe.

Mission to Save the World from Evil Commander Nickelby completed.

DEPARTMENT OF SECURITY AND PROTECTION
OFFICE OF THE DEPARTMENT HEAD
HEXAGON, NEW VANADIUM CITY, V 23

CONFIDENTIAL MEMORANDUM

TO: Charles Coppervitz
            President, HueManTech Inc.

FROM: Mallory Cobaltstein
          Second-in Command, Robothood of Progress

RE: Project Human Race

This is to advise you that Phase I of Project Human Race is officially complete. The Robothood of Progress is in posssesion of a sufficient amount of cellulators from Prototype Unit A, previously known as HueManTech unit #ETC-420-GX-2, to proceed to the next stage. A hand-picked team of technicians at the Departmment of Security and Protection are working with HueManTech technicians around the clock to decipher the genetic code. Once we've broken it, we'll be able to re-create Unit A precisely and freely. Dr. Tinsmith's invention is remarkably efficient and easy to reproduce.

In regard to the events of yesterday, I have launched a full investigation into how the Hexagon's advanced security measures proved incapable of ceasing and desisting a rescue mission coordinated by a civilian minor, identified as Henry Jacobson, 27 Hard Drive, Sodium Falls, NA11. A complete report will not be available until the Nickelby hard drive variant B is installed in the Nickelby clone variant C. Initial findings are detailed in the attached report. As far as the Mainframe is aware, the break-in was perpetrated by an underground terrorist organization. I have manufactured evidence to support this theory, which officials from the Mainframe and the Motherboard find convincing. I expect no trouble on that front.

The commencement of Phase II is a very exciting time for all of us in the Robothood of Progress, and I am confident that with this unexpected development, we will be able to build a SmartHueMan in the immediate future. The revolution has begun!

Please don't hesitate to contact my secretary, Mr. Jeffrey Dubniumwood, ext 363, with any questions. As usual, the passphrase is *a better world for you and me.*

CHAPTER TWENTY
MEGAMAN

On Tinsmith's instructions, they went to Promethium Bounds, a small suburb a few miles west of New Vanadium City with the same neat, little clapboard houses as Sodium Falls. They sought shelter with Oscar Osmiumbaum, an old friend who had gone to the Vanadium Institute of Technology with the famous inventor. He'd helped Tinsmith fake his death forty years ago and was the only bot who knew he was alive.

Osmiumbaum didn't want to take them in. Four decades ago he'd been a lowly swatter on the Reclamation branch of the Circuit Tree with nothing to lose and had signed without qualm the certificate verifying the reuse of the dead inventor's components. But now he was the assistant department head for the Department of Trust, which oversaw quality control of all robot models, and had many qualms. He was an important bot with an important job; if the information that he'd falsified an official document leaked, his brilliant career would be over.

"Dead robots are supposed to stay dead," Oscar said grumpily when he answered the door.

Tinsmith smiled. "Sometimes it doesn't work out that way."

Osmiumbaum harumphed loudly but stepped aside to let them in. Henry collapsed gratefully onto the couch. He was completely wiped out and knew if he shuttered his sight sensors now, he'd switch directly into SLEEP mode. E slid onto the couch next to him, his face still chalky white. Black, purple and yellow marks, fat and oddly shaped, dotted his arms and legs. Henry thought they looked sickly and wanted to contact E's service provider. But Tinsmith *was* his service provider and he assured him E was fine. Even E insisted it was no big deal. He pointed to a bruise around his eye and said he was calling it a shiner because it looked like a tintelage treatment from the Shine Bar.

Henry was also worried about his grandfather. The inventor had gotten more than a few dents in his run-in with Nickelby and had a gash in his left arm. Tinsmith brushed off Henry's concerns, insisting it was nothing a little buff couldn't fix. Some bolts were loose too, and he tightened them as he related their story.

"This won't do. This really won't do," said Ossiumbaum when he discovered they were responsible for Nickelby's death. "I'm sorry to be rude, but you have to vacate these premises immediately."

No one moved, except Tinsmith, who smiled. He didn't seem at all worried by his old friend's attitude.

"This isn't a joking matter. There is a nationwide bot hunt on for Nickelby's slayers," Oscar said impatiently, with a paranoid glance at the door as if expecting a squad of G-bots to burst in. "I can't be found harboring a group of terrorbots.

Do you realize what that would do to my reelection? My opponents would say I'm soft on crime. Please go and leave through the back door. They could be watching the house."

"Hay, we're not terrorbots!" Henry shouted angrily.

"Yeah," seconded E.

"Let's all calm down," Tinsmith said, his voice modulator turned to SOOTHE THE SAVAGE BEASTBOT. "We are not a terrorist organization, which you know very well, and we haven't been followed. Now tell us what's going on."

Osmiumbaum tore his gaze from the door, though his sight sensors darted to it every few seconds. "The Robothood of Peace attacked the Hex and took out Nickelby. It's all over the news. Every channel has the story."

"That's absurd," Tinsmith said. "The ROP hasn't existed for forty years."

"They're back now and apparently sitting in my living room," Osmiumbaum said. "Now please be good guests and skedaddle. I can't harbor fugitives."

"We're not fugitives," Henry said again, agitated at the thought of being thought of as a terrorist. He just *saved* his grandfather and his best friend's life *and* all of Vanadium.

"It's only a story, Henry," Tinsmith insisted. "Nobody is looking for us. The Mainframe had to put out some explanation for Nickelby's death. Even if Mallory Cobaltstein, the head of the Department of Security and Protection, knows what really happened, which I doubt, she couldn't very well admit that the national hero was killed by a long-dead robot and an illegally detained minor. Nor can the Mainframe admit that Nickelby was rotten to the core. No, they need a convenient fiction and resurrecting the Robothood of Peace serves that purpose very nicely. I expected something like this. Trust me, Henry, without Nickelby leading the group, the resurrection, however far it extended, is over. Now, my dear friend Oscar, may I please have some buff cream for my cut?"

"I don't have any," Osmuimbaum said sulkily, probably, Henry thought, because he knew Tinsmith spoke the truth. "And I can't go get any. Everything's closed. It's a national day of mourning."

Tinsmith demanded food instead and stood over Oscar as he capacitated the coal. E popped six MARFELs and washed them down with hydration fluid. After dinner, their host led Henry and E to a guest room with twin beds and florette curtains. He offered E a cardboard box to sleep in, but the human said he much preferred a bed. This statement baffled the assistant department head, who quickly said good night.

As soon as he left, Henry and E fell onto the bed and reviewed every single thing that happened since the moment they were separated. E went first because he didn't have much to tell.

"Nickelby tried to run experiments on me, but I played dumb," he said. "When he gave me a crossword puzzle, I colored in the boxes. When he gave me a book to scan, I tore up the pages. When he gave me a calculator, I sat on it," he said. "It drove him bonkers. He thought there was some trick to operating me that he couldn't figure out. It was pretty funny."

Henry knew he was trying to make light of it, but he wouldn't let him. "Did he hurt you?"

E shrugged. "The really painful part was the benumbing boredom. I tried to scan the book he gave me, but I'd torn the pages too well. That's a lesson you only need to learn once." When Henry didn't return his smile, he said, "Hey, get this: triskaidekaphobia, gobbledygook, antidisestablishmentarianism."

"Huh?" Henry asked.

"My new words. Nifty, right? I've got a ton more. I haven't figured out how to use most of them yet, but it'll come to me. So your turn. Take it from when the glass door closed on the habitatus. Go."

Henry's tale took more than two hours, with E constantly interrupting to ask more questions. By the time Henry was done, the human could barely keep his eyes open. He opened his mouth wide and expelled air, a sure sign that he was about to drop into SLEEP mode. Henry suggested they go to bed and pick up the discussion in the morning.

E agreed, putting his head down, but a moment later he said, "It's weird."

Henry stared at the ceiling. "What?"

"To have the answers. It's like...I don't know...like I can breathe easily for the first time in my life. Does that make sense?"

"Not really but yeah," Henry said truthfully. "Does knowing your past help?"

"You mean with the future?" E asked.

"Yeah."

"That's weird too. I know I have one, but I don't know what it is."

"I do," Henry said with quiet emphasis. "You're coming home with me. Tinsmith can have the back room and you can share mine."

"That sounds great," E said.

"Yeah, and you'll go to school with me because you need to learn stuff too," Henry explained.

"That's true," E said. "There's tons I don't know."

"You'll be in my class. We have Mrs. Yitteriumski. She's all right, but her tutorials are really long and she goes on and on about the most boring topics and her voice modulator is set permanently to LULL SEWING MACHINES TO SLEEP. But don't worry. We'll pass notes to make the time go quicker."

E yawned again. "I can't wait to pass notes."

"But they won't be stupid notes cause passing stupid notes is stupid. So we have to come up with something really important to write about. I know! We'll create our own superhero. We can make him a human like you and called him MegaHuman. No, MegaMan. What do you think of that?"

E muttered something unintelligible and Henry looked over to see that his friend was fast asleep. Happily thinking up adventures for MegaMan, Henry switched his own system to SLEEP mode and shuttered his sight sensors.

In the morning, E and his grandfather were gone.

CHAPTER TWENTY-ONE
Home

Henry stood on the sidewalk in front of his house. For the most part, it looked the same. The front door was open, and his mother's dusk-blooming nightlights swayed gently in the fall breeze. The tourmaline was bright green, perhaps a little rougher than usual, and he felt that if he only listened carefully enough he would hear the sound of his father's shaver.

Someone had closed his bedroom window while he was away, he noticed. For some reason that surprised him, even though he knew it shouldn't. He'd been gone a week—of couse they'd shut it.

A shiny blue car drove by and Mrs. Zincfield slowed the vehicle as she spotted him, making Henry aware he couldn't stand there all day. As soon she parked the car, she'd call his parents to get the lowdown on Henry's reappearance.

He should really go inside before that happened.

But he wasn't ready to yet.

Some of his reluctance was plain old fear of consequences. He knew you didn't get to jump out of your bedroom window and disappear for a week without some awful punishment befalling you. But it was more than that. Going inside meant going back—to his benumbing life, to his friendless existence.

It was stupid to hesitate. His grand human adventure was already over. E and Tinsmith were miles away. Where, Henry didn't know. Tinsmith refused to say in the note Henry had found that morning. "The technology contained within Ethan will always frighten some and tempt others with its possibilities," he'd written, "and so for his own good and for yours, he must disappear. Don't worry. I'll keep him safe. In my absence, I'm counting on you to do the same for my son. I know he's in good hands. You are a hero, Henry. Even if you never get a Vanadium Metal of Distinction, you are a hero in every sense of the word."

E also left a note. He apologized to Henry for sneaking out. He knew it was wrong, but saying good-bye face-to-face would've been too hard. "I would've wanted to stay and I can't. I would only hurt you and your parents. Tinsmith is taking me far, far away to a place where I won't hurt anyone. And you have a life to get back to. I can never thank you enough for all you've done. Thank you for believing in my humanity. Thank you for saving my life. Thank you for being my friend. Your best, best, best buddy, E."

He added a PS saying he couldn't wait to see the first issue of MegaMan comic on the newsstand and a PPS promising to see him again. Henry knew neither one would ever happen but especially the second. It was too dangerous.

A few houses down, Mrs. Zincfield's car door slammed. A soft breeze stirred; the nightlights fluttered.

The green lawn waited to be shaved, and Henry Jacobson spun around, finding it all too familiar to bear.

He took one step, then another, then he was racing down the block to the corner, around the corner, a left onto Disk Drive. He didn't know where he was going; he didn't care. Anywhere but here, he thought. Anything but this.

The red light at Disk Drive and Main Street stopped him and suddenly he was in front of the Shine Bar and he was staring at his own reflection. He looked exactly the same. Of course he did. Did he really expect to look different?

But he *was* different. Maybe not on the outside but on the inside. The *wzzz-wzzz* that had plagued him for almost half his life was gone, replaced by a soft *whrrr-whrrr* that he could control. The tormenting bug was finally vanquished. And that wasn't all. The greatest hero turned evil villian the world had ever seen had been vanquished too—by him. He, Henry Jacobson, aka Hank Lank, aka the most useless kid in all of Sodium Falls Middle School, had charged into the bowels of the Hex and saved robotkind.

He didn't run then; he couldn't run now.

Slowly, he turned from the window, from Disk Drive and the traffic light and retraced his steps. In a matter of minutes he was standing again in front of his house, but this time he didn't stop at the curb to look in. He strolled up the path lined with nightlights, pushed open the door that was unlocked as always and called out to his parents.

He was home.

ABOUT THE AUTHOR

L.A. MESSINA is the author of several novels. She lives in New York City with her husband and sons.